DACHSHUND THROUGH THE SNOW

THE DOGMOTHERS - BOOK THREE

roxanne st. claire

Dachshund Through the Snow
THE DOGMOTHERS BOOK THREE

Copyright © 2019 South Street Publishing

ISBN Print: 978-1-7339121-8-1
ISBN Ebook: 978-1-7339121-7-4

COVER DESIGN: Keri Knutson
INTERIOR FORMATTING: Author EMS

Critical Reviews of Roxanne St. Claire Novels

"Non-stop action, sweet and sexy romance, lively characters, and a celebration of family and forgiveness."
— *Publishers Weekly*

"Plenty of heat, humor, and heart!"
— *USA Today* (Happy Ever After blog)

"Beautifully written, deeply emotional, often humorous, and always heartwarming!"
— *The Romance Dish*

"Roxanne St. Claire is the kind of author that will leave you breathless with tears, laughter, and longing as she brings two people together, whether it is their first true love or a second love to last for all time."
— *Romance Witch Reviews*

"Roxanne St. Claire writes an utterly swoon-worthy romance with a tender, sentimental HEA worth every emotional struggle her readers will endure. Grab your tissues and get ready for some ugly crying. These books rip my heart apart and then piece it back together with the hope, joy and indomitable loving force that is the Kilcannon clan."
— *Harlequin Junkies*

"As always, Ms. St. Claire's writing is perfection…I am unable to put the book down until that final pawprint the end. Oh the feels!"
— *Between My BookEndz*

Before
The Dogmothers...
there was

Sit…Stay…Beg (Book 1)
New Leash on Life (Book 2)
Leader of the Pack (Book 3)
Santa Paws is Coming to Town (Book 4 – a Holiday novella)
Bad to the Bone (Book 5)
Ruff Around the Edges (Book 6)
Double Dog Dare (Book 7)
Bark! The Herald Angels Sing – (Book 8 – a Holiday novella)
Old Dog New Tricks (Book 9)

Find information and buy links for all these books here:
http://www.roxannestclaire.com/dogfather-series

For a complete guide to all of the characters in both The
Dogfather and Dogmothers series, see the back of this
book. Or visit www.roxannestclaire.com for a printable
reference, book lists, buy links, and reading order of all my
books. Be sure to sign up for my newsletter to find out
when the next book is released! And join the private
Dogfather Facebook group for inside info on all the books
and characters, sneak peeks, and a place to share the love of
tails and tales!

www.facebook.com/groups/roxannestclairereaders/

Chapter One

"Agnes Santorini, my dear lass." Finnie clapped her hands in front of her face with a gleam in her blue eyes not even her thick bifocals could hide. "I have good news, and I have bad news."

"I don't want bad news on Christmas Eve, Finnie." Agnes gave the Christopsomo dough a solid knead with her knuckles. "So skip that part and tell me what's good."

"All righty, then." Finnie peered at her phone, which Agnes knew was so magnified it barely showed four letters on the screen at a time. "It's a text from my son, Daniel. He says, 'Tell Yiayia that we have just gotten word that a man in town named Rad Shepherd'—"

"Are you reading that right? What kind of dumb name is Rad?"

Finnie looked up, a familiar chastisement in her expression. "Agnes, you're slipping back to yer old self a wee bit frequently."

Agnes made a face. "Damn...er, darn. I know. Okay, okay."

"Don't mean to pester, Agnes, but ye asked me for a

1

remindin' to smooth out the sharp edges. Now, most of the time, your wit is just a nice edge. But sometimes, it cuts."

"Got it." Agnes's cheeks warmed, knowing she was right. "And you're not pestering."

"Good. And let me add that Shepherd seems like a very fine name indeed, especially on Christmas Eve."

"Now, what's the good news, Finola? If it means more baking, I need to get to it."

"No baking. The good news is that this Rad Shepherd has a dachshund you can buy from him."

"A dachshund?" At the pitch of excitement in her voice and the familiar word, both dogs of that very same breed jumped up from their naps and barked, sensing something big was afoot. And it was.

"A brown, short-hair, two-year-old doxie," Finnie said.

No! That was it! That very dachshund who…she shook off the thought. "Are you sure?" Agnes sidled around the counter to seize the phone from Finnie's hands, blinking at what had to be seventy-three-point font. "How on earth do you read texts like this?"

"Much more easily than on your phone." Finnie gave her an elbow jab. "Be nice. Last warning."

"So this guy acquired the dog from his dead uncle and wants to unload it?" she asked after reading Daniel's message.

Finnie frowned. "I'm certain those weren't my son's words."

"But that's what he means. Let's go." She shoved the phone back into Finnie's hand. "Let's go get the dog. Whatever he wants. Money. Cookies. Hell, I'll sleep with the man."

2

"Agnes Santorini! You are eighty years old."

Eighty-two, but hey, what's a few years among friends? "I need that dog, Finnie. And not one of that breed has come through your family's canine business."

"Well, there was that long-hair tan one I loved."

Not long hair. Not tan. It had to match her memory. "But that was not the dog of my...dreams."

Finnie tsked and reached down to pet Gala's head. "She loves you, too, lass."

"Oh please, Galatea and Pygmalion know I worship the ground they poop on. But..." There was another one out there whom she *had to have*. Brown with short hair. She could close her eyes and see his face, clear as a bell, as the memory of that...that *trip*...would forever be in her mind. She could still feel the air, see the light, and remember the word she'd heard over and over again. *Charis*.

"And boy or girl, its name will be..." *Charis*.

"Didn't you read the end of the text?" Finnie asked. "'Tis a boy, already named Rover."

"*Rover?*" She almost choked. "Is that a joke? Why not just call him Boy Dog? That has to be the most unimaginative, stupid, pathetic—"

One of Finnie's white brows lifted. "He's not so busy on Christmas Eve that He can't hear what you say and how you say it," she said softly, clearing up her brogue so the reminder came in loud and clear.

Agnes made a face. "Something tells me that you don't mean Santa Claus."

Finnie fought a smile at the quip, but it faded quickly. "Aye, but speaking of Santa Claus, that's the bad news."

3

"Hasn't got the sleigh packed yet?" she joked.

"He left town."

"Excuse me?"

"George Snodgrass, the man who has been playing Santa Clause to my Mrs. Claus all week at the Winter Wonderland Festival in Bushrod Square? His kids surprised him with tickets to New York, and he's gone."

"Just like a man," Agnes grumbled. "You have one more night to do the festival, and it's Christmas Eve, for heaven's sake. How could he just up and leave you to find a Santa substitute on the night the children are going to sit on his lap and get gifts?"

"Well, he did, and we have no lap. Not a lap to be found tonight. Every lap in Bitter Bark is spoken for."

"None of the other men in town can step in?"

"Not on Christmas Eve," Finnie said as she walked out of the kitchen. "They're either already involved with the festival, or doing the big play tonight at First Baptist, or committed to family."

"Well, that's a shame." Agnes eyed the dough, trying to decide if she should finish this bread quickly, or just start from scratch after she had Charis.

"But I did come up with a solution," Finnie called from the dining room.

"Oh, good. So, I think we should—"

She stopped midword when Finnie returned with an armload of red velvet and white fur, lifting it high and offering a look that Agnes already knew far too well.

"Not a chance, Finola Kilcannon."

"Mrs. Claus needs a husband, Agnes."

"Who doesn't? But I'm not going to be yours."

"'Tis two hours of your evening. You'll do nothin' but sit next to me, be kind to children, and I'll hand them a present from the pile."

"I do not look like a fat old man from the North Pole. I've dieted my heart out and stuck enough Botox in my face to smooth the face of a shar-pei. I will not—"

Finnie stuck a giant white cotton ball in Agnes's face. "Wear this beard and ho-ho-ho your heart out." Her tone invited no arguments. "We'll be finished early enough to head to Waterford Farm for the big celebration, the placement of the candle in the window, followed by gift giving, then Midnight Mass."

"The fun never stops."

Finnie wiggled the beard and lifted a brow that was nearly the same shade of white. "You want me to agree to a third dog in our house?"

"Finnie! You said—"

"Then polish up your ho-ing, and I don't mean the dirty kind." She gave a toothsome grin. "You know it'll be fun, lass."

Agnes gave her a look. "I'm not a lass."

"Then you should have no problem playing Santa to my Mrs."

With an angry sniff, Agnes took the red costume and held up the red jacket. "And I'm not fat enough to play this part."

"Why God invented pillows."

Oh good heavens. Hadn't she lost twenty percent of herself last year so she didn't look like she was padded with pillows? "On one condition."

"Name it."

"We get to bring my new dog."

Finnie considered that, then nodded. "I knitted a few elf hats for all the family dogs for our picture tonight," she said. "I have an extra one that Rover can—"

"He will *not* be called Rover." He would be Charis, but she had no intention of explaining all that to Finnie.

Finnie, ever the fine negotiator, tilted her head in concession. "Then all three doxies can come with us to the festival and be part of our act."

Victorious, she closed her eyes and saw the image of the dog she'd been searching for since…that day. Maybe this was the one. Maybe this was Charis.

Just then, the back door opened, and Prudence, Finnie's teenage great-granddaughter, stepped in, her creamy cheeks pink and her eyes bright from cold as she rubbed her hands together. "I'm here to help you bake, Yiayia," she announced, bending over to greet the dogs when they bounded toward her.

"Baking can wait," Agnes said. "There's more important work to do."

"More important than baking?" Pru shot Finnie a pretend look of shock. "Has she been hitting the ouzo early?"

"No, lass, but…" Finnie's brows furrowed as she walked closer to Pru. "I thought you were supposed to work the ornament table with the other high school volunteers at the festival."

"Yeah…well." She dropped her head to snuggle Pyggie. "Hey there, handsome little man. You look like you lost a pound or two."

"Pru."

She glanced up. "Sorry, Gramma. I know he's sensitive about his weight." She looked around Finnie's narrow frame to catch Agnes's eye. "You might have thought of that when you gave him the name, Yiayia."

"What's the matter?" Finnie asked, ignoring the exchange and laser-focused on Pru.

"Nothing," she said, with just enough hesitation to make Agnes doubt that was true.

"You've been crying," Finnie said.

Guilt flashed over her young and pretty features. "No, I haven't. It's just…"

"Cold," Agnes suggested, feeling the inexplicable need to help the girl out.

"Exactly. It's going to snow some more," she said with false brightness. "Nothing like snow on Christmas Eve. So what are we baking, Yiayia? That Christo… Greek Christmas bread?"

She tried to slide past Finnie to get to the counter, but the tiny woman stepped to the side and put a finger up. "Lass, I know you better than yer own mirror. What's gotcha, my child?"

Pru opened her mouth to say something, then shut it, closing her eyes and shaking her head. "I don't want to talk about it. I want to bake with my two favorite grannies in the whole world. That's what's fun. That's what's…*cool*." Her voice almost cracked, but she recovered with a huge grin. "Teach me everything you know, Yiayia."

Agnes's old heart shifted. "I think you've got some Greek in you, *koukla*."

"Aww, that's what you call Cassie," she said, referring to Agnes's one and only granddaughter.

"But we can't bake," Agnes said. "Not for a while."

"'Tis true," Finnie added. "We have a very important errand to run. We're off to the home of Rad Shepherd."

7

"Rad?" Pru choked a laugh. "Like, his name is Radical? That's pretty dumb."

Agnes shot an *I told you so* look to Finnie.

"And why are we going there?" Pru asked.

"Because he has my Christmas present," Agnes told her, feeling the smile pull at her face. "The very thing I've been waiting for and wanting for such a long time."

"That third dachshund you keep talking about?" Pru guessed.

"That's it," Agnes confirmed, pleased that the young girl knew her that well. "The dachshund of my dreams." *Literally.*

"Come on, you two," Finnie said, turning to the coat-tree to get her jacket. "Leash the dogs, and let's go."

"Uh…how are we getting there?" Pru asked. "Yiayia's Buick is in the shop getting new brakes, remember? My overprotective father won't let me get a learner's permit until spring. And, Gramma, you are not driving on Christmas Eve again. Remember last year?"

She paled a little. "Aye. 'Twas a misadventure in the snowy mountains we dare not repeat. So, we're going to walk."

"*Walk?*" Agnes's and Pru's responses came out in perfect unison. And, of course, the dogs ran in circles at the word *walk*.

"'Tis a short stroll on a fine Christmas Eve day," Finnie said, looking at her phone. "I have our good Shepherd's address right here. We can walk directly through the square and see all the festivities about. We'll be back here in no time, with a new dachshund and a full day of baking—and barking—ahead of us."

8

"It's awfully chilly to walk," Agnes said, putting a hand over the heart she was never sure would make it to the next hour, let alone the next day.

"And do we have to go through the square?" Pru asked. "I've had just about enough of that place today."

Finnie turned from the door, looking from one to the other. "Agnes," she said. "Yer ticker will benefit from a wee bit of exercise. Use it or lose it. And, Prudence, my darlin', whatever drama is unfolding with the high school lassies, yer best to face it head-on."

Pru's jaw loosened, and she looked at Agnes. "How does she do that? How does she know?"

"She's a canny one," Agnes agreed.

"I know the people I love, 'tis all." Finnie fussed at her feathery white hair with a bit of pride in her blue eyes. "Now, let's get a move on it, ladies. Oh, and, Agnes, tell Pru who's going to play Santa Claus tonight at the festival."

"Please, I almost forgot my punishment. Ho ho, oh no."

"*You* are?" Pru almost choked with a bubbling laugh. "Where's George Snodgrass?"

"New York, the old bas..."

"*Agnes.*"

"Bas...bass fisherman," she quickly corrected with a wink to Pru. "He's gone off to see his family, like it's Christmas or something."

Pru laughed and held up a hand for a high five. "You'll be a great Santa. Now let's go get...what's the new dog's name?"

"Rover," Finnie said before Agnes could open her mouth.

"Rover?" Pru threw a lock back of long black hair in disbelief. "Someone actually named a dog *Rover*?"

"I knew I liked this girl." Agnes slipped into her coat and found her handbag, checking to see if her wallet was there, because she'd pay whatever *Rad*ical wanted. "Whatever we call him…" *And it will be Charis.* "He'll be a Christmas miracle for me."

They stepped out into the brisk North Carolina day, locking arms to walk over last night's dusting of snow, with Pyggie and Gala prancing on leashes in the lead. Well, Pyggie was waddling in the lead, but they'd get there eventually, and then they'd bring home the dachshund that would save Agnes's life.

Chapter Two

P ru tried to listen to the two grannies chatter as they walked down Dogwood Lane toward the heart of Bitter Bark, but she was still replaying every word that had just been exchanged with Teagan Macdonald, her best friend. Well, her *former* best friend.

"Can we take the long way around Bushrod Square?" she suggested as they neared the square-mile park that was currently overrun with all things holiday. "It's so crowded with...revelers."

"And add all that time to our walk?" Yiayia scoffed and gestured toward the candy cane arches that led to the statue of Thaddeus Ambrose Bushrod, the town's founder. "Not a chance when my doxie is waiting."

Pru squished her nose and went with them, tucking her face into the fake fur collar of her parka and keeping her eyes on the two dogs who marched past brightly lit bushes into the square.

"So, who ya hidin' from, lass?" Gramma nudged her lightly.

"A boy?" Yiayia asked.

"Not likely," Gramma responded for her when Pru stayed quiet. "If I know my Prudence, and I do, this tiff's about the lassies."

She let out a noisy sigh. "Gramma's right," she admitted. "And not really lass*ies*, but one in particular." She glanced from one to the other. "Teagan was really awful."

"Teagan?" Gramma Finnie said. "The pretty one with the reddish hair and curls? Why, she's too Irish to be unkind. I very much like that lass."

"Well, I very much liked her, too, until she made me feel like a pariah at the ornament-decorating booth." Pru glanced in the general direction of the fundraising tables. "She and Sarah and Caitlin, who I hate, by the way, were just whispering and laughing and acting like I wasn't even there."

"Don't hate anyone," Yiayia said. "It'll come back to haunt you."

"Well, I intensely dislike her with every fiber of my being. It's bad enough that Sarah practically had her tongue down Drew Irving's throat when I got there, then Caitlin is waving around this necklace that I guarantee you she didn't pay for."

"A gift?" Gramma asked.

"A five-finger discount." She made a "plucking and pocketing" gesture.

"Are you sure?" Gramma's voice rose in surprise.

"That's quite an allegation," Yiayia said.

Pru just shook her head, not in any mood to defend those girls. She didn't care about them. But Teagan? "My best friend just took off with them, even though we had lunch planned for weeks. We were going to exchange gifts, but Teagan acted like I made up the whole thing and we were never going anywhere. I've never, ever known her to be mean like that. She acted like the idea of Christmas presents was something only five-year-olds like her little sister would do with friends. I mean, come *on*."

The memory still burned, especially the way Teagan and the other two had walked away without even saying goodbye, like a pack of mean girls, leaving Pru standing all alone until the next ornament-making shift arrived. She'd had no choice but to walk to Gramma and Yiayia's house off the square since she didn't have a ride home until Mom got off duty at her vet office. And that could be hours because she was dealing with a cat in a troubled labor.

"I don't know what's going on with her, lass, but I hope you make up," Gramma said. "You know, a good friend is like a four-leaf clover—hard to find and lucky to have."

Pru had to work not to roll her eyes. Usually, her grandmother's silly Irish sayings were cute and funny, but nothing was cute and funny today.

Yiayia leaned into her. "Perhaps something personal is going on and she doesn't want to have a conversation with you about it."

Pru considered that, but she couldn't imagine what Teagan would do that she wouldn't share, unless Caitlin had taken her "shopping."

"She started acting weird about a week ago, but today was off the charts."

"Maybe you can call her after we get the dog," Yiayia suggested.

"Take the high road," Gramma Finnie chimed in.

"'Tis always the right path, most especially on Christmas Eve."

Pru managed a nod, but she had no intention of calling Teagan. Not after the way she'd been treated. So she kept her head down as they walked through the crowds, with Gala and Pyggie occasionally barking at the other dogs that passed through Bushrod Square.

"On the way back, I'll have another doxie," Yiayia said in a happy voice. Then she whispered to Pru, "And you don't have to call anyone if you don't want to make amends."

"Me make amends?" Pru snorted. "She needs to grovel, or I'm keeping that beautiful blue sweater she loved so much last time we went shopping. She nearly cried for how bad she wanted it, and right now it's wrapped in a box in Mom's office. You know, I think I'll wear it tomorrow for Christmas. No, no. I'm going to wear it to school the first day after break. That'll show her."

"Prudence." Gramma Finnie patted her arm. "Bitter is not a nice taste in your mouth, lass."

She shot a look at Yiayia, who shrugged. "Sometimes it is," Yiayia said under her breath. "In the right recipe."

Pru didn't answer as they worked their way past some dancing elves and around the entrance to the Christmas train that ran the perimeter of the square all through December.

Gramma eyed her as they reached the other side and started down Ambrose Avenue. "I think you should talk to her and find out what's in her heart before you end a perfectly lovely friendship."

14

"I still think she should think twice before she's mean, spiteful, and rejects her best friend."

Yiayia let it go as they walked the rest of the distance in silence, stopping occasionally because Gramma Finnie saw a friend, or to let faster pedestrians go by, or even admire a Christmas display in a store window. Just off the main street of town, they headed into a residential area and found the small house with the address Gramma Finnie had in her phone.

"Let me do the talking," Yiayia announced as they slowed in front of the driveway. "And don't talk me out of whatever he wants for the dog. I have the money."

"A dachshund shouldn't be that expensive," Pru said.

Yiayia gave her a hard look. "You can't put a price on how much I want this dog. Of course, he has to look...a certain way. If he doesn't..." Her voice trailed off.

Pru made a face. "Pretty sure you've been hanging around the Kilcannons long enough to know beauty is in the eye of the beholder where dogs are concerned." She tipped her head. "Like, look at Pyggie."

The chubby little pup wagged his tail at the mention of his name.

"This dog needs to look...like I imagine him to look."

Pru frowned and glanced at Gramma Finnie for some help on this. "Like you imagine him to look?"

Gramma shrugged as if she'd had this conversation and gotten nowhere.

"Just...let me do the talking," Yiayia said, giving Gala's leash to Pru. "You two stay a little behind with the dogs so we can give them a chance to get acquainted."

She took a few steps ahead to the door, then rang the bell. Instantly, a dog started frantically barking from behind the door, which set off Pyggie and Gala, too. The racket was deafening, but funny.

"Yes, that sounds like a doxie," Yiayia said on a high-pitched laugh.

After a moment, the front door was opened by a balding man who looked to be about fifty, holding a squirming brown dog in his arms. "Can I help you?"

"Oh my sweet heavens alive!" Yiayia exclaimed. "It's Charis!"

Charis? Pru and Gramma Finnie exchanged a look, but didn't attempt to talk over the cacophony of three dachshunds barking.

"It's Rover," the man said, eyeing her suspiciously. "Can I help you?"

"I'm here to buy your dachshund," Yiayia announced. "Please tell me it's that one right there in your arms and that you are really willing to part with him."

"I am," he said, opening the door wider, silently inviting her in. "Come on in. Your friends, too, assuming they don't bite."

Yiayia laughed, more excited than Pru had ever seen her. "Only the one with white hair," she joked.

The ice broken, they all headed in, banging some snow from their boots while Pru held the leashes tight so the dogs could get used to the place. They stood in a small entryway, a Christmas tree visible on a table in the living room and two stockings both embroidered with an *R* hanging from the fireplace mantel. For

Rover and Rad? He had a stocking for a dog he was selling?

The whole house was sparse and dim, like an air of sadness hung over it instead of Christmas cheer.

"Can I hold him?" Yiayia asked, reaching greedily for Rover.

"Of course," he said. "He's a good dog, but he just doesn't get along with Ralph."

"Ralph?" Yiayia looked past him, as if expecting to see another man. His father? Son? Maybe a cat who fought with dogs?

He gestured for them to step into the living room, and there, in a huge glass tank that looked like it could house a cow, was a giant lizard. It had to be almost two feet long, with spots all over his back and pinkish spikes poking out from his chin.

"Oh my!" Gramma Finnie jumped back, even though it was enclosed in glass. Yiayia let out a shriek of surprise. Both dogs barked, but instantly backed away as if sensing that they weren't in charge here.

But Pru gasped as she realized what it was. "A bearded dragon!" she exclaimed, aching to reach for it. "I've been begging my mother for one of these."

"This is Ralph," he said. "He belonged to my wife, but she's..." He heaved a sigh. "She's gone home."

"Oh, lad." Gramma reached out. "You have my sympathies. Such a hard time of year to mourn a lost loved one."

"She's not lost," he said quickly. "She literally went home. To live with her mother. The old bag lives in Arizona."

Gramma Finnie drew back, and Pru bit her lip to keep from laughing at the way he said it.

"So, which of you ladies is getting Rover?"

"I am," Yiayia said, nuzzling her head into the dog's fur, the connection between them instant. "He's perfect. Absolutely perfect."

"So you want him?" the man asked.

"With my whole heart and soul," she crooned, holding him up to gaze into his big brown eyes. "I want you, sweet thing. Oh yes, I do!"

Of course, Pyggie and Gala barked possessively at the baby talk, tugging on their leashes to let this intruder know exactly who Yiayia *really* loved.

"It's okay," Pru assured them.

"It sure is," Yiayia said, lowering Rover so he could be closer to the other two doxies. "This is going to be your new brother!"

"Well, I do have a price that you'll have to pay."

"Of course. I brought my checkbook." Yiayia tapped the bag hanging on her shoulder. "How much are you asking?"

He looked from one to the other, gnawing his lip. With each second that ticked by, Pru got a little anxious. Was he going to demand an astronomical amount of money? Would Yiayia pay it?

"I want a ticket to the First Baptist Christmas Spectacular event."

Pru blinked at the request. Gramma Finnie let out a soft hoot. And Yiayia drew back in disbelief.

"You might as well ask for a seat on the moon," she said with a snort. "I've heard that if there's a ticket to be had, it's selling for more money than God makes."

Pru couldn't argue with that. The two-act Christmas extravaganza that all the churches in town got together to produce at First Baptist of Bitter Bark had been sold out since September. They'd had performances all week, but Christmas Eve was the biggie, with a live baby Jesus at the end of the first act and the promise of real reindeer in the second.

"Well, that's my price," he said, angling his head with a hint of smugness, as if he could sense the dog meant a lot. "I've never missed the show, not once, but my wife was the one who got the tickets. She didn't this year, then she left and..." He shook his head. "It's not Christmas for me if I don't see that performance."

"Well, that's just the stupidest thing I ever heard," Yiayia said, earning a soft gasp from Gramma Finnie, who believed in speaking her mind, but never quite as bluntly as her closest friend. "You'll just have to miss it one year. I'm willing to pay cash, and maybe you can find a scalper."

He shook his head. "A ticket...for a decent seat, not nosebleeds," he replied with so much determination, Pru could practically hear his heels digging into the hardwood floor. "That's my price."

Yiayia grunted in frustration.

"Wait a second," Gramma Finnie said softly. "I *might* be able to help."

Yiayia whipped around, and the man looked just as interested. "How?" they asked in unison.

"One of the men from St. Gabriel's, which is my church, is workin' as the set director for the play at First Baptist. I know this because I begged him to be Santa Claus tonight," she added as an aside to Yiayia. "When he turned that down, he offered so kindly to help me out in any other way he could. Such a good man, he—"

"Call him," Yiayia said. "He'll have a ticket. He *has* to have a ticket."

Rad stepped closer and lifted Rover right out of Yiayia's arms. "If I get the ticket, you get the dog," he said.

Yiayia gave him a look Pru rarely saw from her, but that she'd certainly heard her Santorini step-cousins and their mother talk about. Like, if looks could kill, poor Rad would be headed to Easterbrook Funeral Home, not the Christmas Spectacular.

"You will give me that dog," she said through gritted teeth. "It's important."

"So's the play," he countered, undaunted by her. "Get me a ticket, and you can have the dog. I'll be here all day, 'cept for taking Rover for a walk. If you can't get the ticket, you can't have the dog."

"Then we'll get a ticket," Yiayia said, signaling for Gramma, Pru, and the dogs to follow her out the front door.

"Bye, Ralph," Pru whispered into the tank, then gave a quick pet to the dog Rad held. "See you, Rover." She looked up at the man. "You drive a hard bargain, dude."

"I want the ticket."

"Got it." Pru zipped out with the two dogs to find Gramma Finnie and Yiayia deep in conversation on the sidewalk. "So, we're going to the church to try and sell our souls for a ticket?"

"Whatever it takes," Gramma Finnie said.

"Thank you." Yiayia put her hand on Gramma's back. "You're a good friend, Finola."

While they trudged back down Ambrose Avenue, Yiayia was silent as Gramma Finnie chatted about her friend Melvin Jankewicz, the set director, and how he could help them. She was certain he'd be at First Baptist all day, so they headed toward the large white columns of the stately church not far from the town hall at the perimeter of Bushrod Square.

"Won't take but a minute to get the ticket," Gramma said.

Yiayia gave a skeptical look over her shoulder in the direction they'd just come from. "Then he better give us that dog when we get back with the ticket and not send us off on another goose chase," she said. "Maybe he's some kind of scam artist."

"A scam to go to a Christmas play?" Gramma Finnie gave a soft snort. "My word, Agnes, you don't trust anyone."

"Life has taught me that," she said. "Life taught me..."

Her words faded in Pru's ear at the outburst of girls' laughter from the square as they passed one of the entrances. The musical cadence of one was all too familiar. She looked to her left and felt a stab of pain at the sight of Teagan huddled with Caitlin, Sarah, and one other girl who ran in that crowd at school.

Just as Pru stared at them, Teagan looked up, a flash of something in her eyes, then she quickly looked away, pretending she hadn't seen Pru.

"Oh..." The sound slipped from Pru's lips, getting a quick look from Yiayia. But Pru didn't say a word because, for all she knew, Yiayia would march under those candy cane arches and demand an explanation from Teagan. "That's...sad," she finished.

21

"What is?" Yiayia asked.

"That life taught you not to trust people." Although, wasn't life grinding that lesson on Pru's heart right then?

"How did that happen, lass?" Gramma asked, sliding a loving hand through Agnes's arm. "Who let you down?"

"Who didn't?" she answered in her wry Yiayia tone. "And on Christmas Day, too."

"Really?" Pru asked.

"Certainly not your husband or children," Gramma said. "Not on Christmas."

The other woman didn't answer for a long time, looking ahead, her eyes pinned on something in the distance. Or a memory.

"What happened?" Pru asked. "Can you share with us?"

Yiayia's eyes shuttered closed, and some color drained from her cheeks. "Oh, I don't know. It's all such ancient history now."

"That's the best kind," Gramma said.

"Last Christmas Eve, Gramma Finnie told me the most amazing story. Now it's your turn."

Yiayia smiled and sighed. "I'm not the storyteller your Irish great-grandmother is."

"You can't share anything about your life?" Pru asked.

"After I've told you so much of mine?" Gramma added.

They took a few more steps, silent. Then Yiayia slowed and finally stopped, tugging at the dogs. "The first person to let me down and break my trust was my father," she said softly. "I walked into the kitchen on

Christmas morning, just a few days after I'd turned eighteen, and he announced that he'd found my husband, a man from Greece who I'd never met."

Pru gasped. "You had an arranged marriage?"

"Not…exactly."

Chapter Three

Astoria, New York, 1955

Agnes opened her eyes and squinted through the tiny slats of her attic window to confirm that it had, indeed, not stopped snowing yet. Which might make a lot of people happy today, Christmas morning, but it meant that Norman's car might not make it all the way to Astoria from the city tomorrow so they could meet and have their secret gift exchange.

Her heart dropped. It was already risky enough meeting the day after Christmas, which was just as much a celebration as any of the other thirteen days between Christmas Eve and the Epiphany, at least if you were Greek. Tomorrow should be called the feast of the sweets, since they'd eat nothing but thiples, kataifi, and baklava, all drizzled with honey and enjoyed with ouzo.

But the only sweet thing that mattered that day to Agnes was Norman.

Yes, the house would be full of family and friends

24

and food, and Agnes would be expected to participate in the holiday traditions. Then again, with her parents so wrapped up with the party, they might not notice if she took a walk for a few hours.

Unless it was snowing and the only way to see him was to take the subway to the city. They'd notice that.

With a sigh, she threw back the blanket and put her bare feet on the cold attic floor, looking at the two other beds in the tiny third-floor bedroom, empty now that both Helen and Irene had moved out. A pang of envy squeezed her heart, not that she was jealous of either of the "good Greek boys" her sisters had met and married.

No, that jolt of jealousy was because they'd escaped the oppressive control of Estevan Mastros, while Agnes remained under the steel hammer of their father. And that hammer was going to come down hard when she told him she'd fallen in love with a man seven years her senior named Norman Anderson.

A little shiver ran over her, and not just because the register up here often broke and wasn't sending out any steam heat.

"Norman Anderson." She smiled as his name rolled over her lips, as delicious as his kisses and as...*not* Greek as any man she'd ever met.

Well, too bad. She was eighteen years old, it was 1955, and she could fall in love with a man who wasn't Greek. And the fact that he was twenty-five? Well, they shouldn't have left her alone here for a weekend, forced to answer the door when a brush salesman knocked and swept her right off her feet. She'd fallen hard for his crooked smile and sweet green eyes and long, lean fingers that drove her crazy when they slipped so close to places on her body he really shouldn't touch...yet.

If Norman couldn't make it here tomorrow, well, then, she'd *walk* all the way to New York City if she had to. There wasn't *anything* she wouldn't do for him...except the one thing he wanted so much.

She'd held him off so far, hoping to wait until they got married. Or at least...engaged. Maybe then she'd give in to his pleas. But they couldn't get engaged until she told her father the truth about him. Well, she told her father the truth *and* Norman popped the question.

But she wouldn't be making her big announcement today, she thought as she straightened her long cotton nightgown. She was going to be a bad Greek daughter very soon, but not so bad she'd ruin her family's Christmas.

Inhaling the aroma of her father's strong coffee that wafted up the two flights of stairs to her room, she skipped slippers and headed straight there, already tasting the cookie she'd dip in her own cup.

She followed the scent and the sound of her father's deep voice as he spoke in Greek to Mama, the words of his native language mostly running together in Agnes's brain.

"Speak English, Baba," she said as she walked into the kitchen. *Norman won't understand a word you're saying.* Not that Estevan Mastros would ever say anything to a non-Greek twenty-five-year-old brush salesman from Indiana who had the audacity to fall in love with Agnes. Not until he got to know how kind and smart Norman was. Then maybe her father would like the man Agnes loved. "You live in America now."

26

He scowled at her from over the rim of his fat white cup. "*Kala Christougenna*, Agnes."

She started to answer in Greek, but something stopped her. A gleam in eyes the color of a ripe black olive, and a...wait a second.

Was her father *smiling*?

The sight was so rare she blinked at him. "Merry Christmas to you, too, Baba," she answered softly, as if speaking too loud in any language might ruin the moment. Glancing at her mother, who'd taken a break from rolling dough at the counter, Agnes *knew* something was up. Mama's dark eyes danced, too, and her dimples were deep. This wasn't just a nice Christmas morning.

"How's everyone?" she asked awkwardly, sliding into a chair and reaching for a kourabiedes. The powdered sugar on the cookie flaked like the snowfall that had started last night while they lit the traditional Christmas boat and sang kalanda, or as Americans called them, Christmas carols.

"Tell her, Estevan," her mother said, coming to the table. "Tell her now. Don't wait for the whole family."

"Tell me what?" she asked, looking from her mother's pretty face to her father's oddly happy one. Baba was rarely happy. This must be important. "Wait," Agnes said around a mouthful of cookie. "Let me guess. Helen's pregnant. Finally." She'd begun to think Cosmo was shooting blanks.

Baba's eyes flashed with something that was probably disappointment, but it disappeared as quickly as it had come. "No baby for Helen yet."

"Then Irene?" she guessed, swallowing the sugary cookie bite. "Mama, can I have coffee?"

Her mother ignored the request and put her hands, strong from kneading dough, on Agnes's shoulders. "Baba has news for you." She tightened her grip, as if this news was so exciting, it might make Agnes pop up from the table.

"What kind of news?"

"Good news," he said. "Very good news, *koukla*."

Koukla? He called her that only on her birthday. Silent, she lowered her cookie and stared at him, her brain zipping through the possibilities. A job? A car? A change of heart about going to secretarial school? Those requests had been scoffed at over the past year, so why would they change?

Not that it mattered now that she had her future planned with Norman, but she was curious what he'd say.

"We have found you a husband."

She blinked at him, a nervous, sickening laugh bubbling up. "A...what?"

Mama's hands pressed harder. "Do you remember the man who does the landscaping in the park? Allessandro Santorini?"

That laugh came out, a little more like a horse's snort. "He's damn near sixty, Mama!"

"Agnes." Her father's reprimand came through in the word, as sharp as if he'd snapped a whip at her. "You do not swear, in any language."

"But that Santorini guy is old!" Of course, if Baba thought that coot was husband material, then twenty-five might not sound so bad when they met Norman. "And I'm not marrying anyone just because you picked him."

His fist came down on the table with a thud so

loud, they had to have heard it in the next row house. "Not him!" her father said. "His nephew, who has just arrived here from Greece. He'll be here tonight for dinner. Nikodemus Théodoro Santorini. He has agreed to a betrothal, and the engagement will begin tonight at midnight."

Each word hit her harder, like repeated slaps that knocked all the ability to think out of her head.

"Baba." She barely whispered the word. "You cannot make me marry some man I've never met."

"I can and I will." He picked up his coffee as if the discussion were over.

"You cannot and you won't. This is 1955, not 1055! This is America, not the old country. And I am old enough to make my own choices, thank you very much."

His eyes shuttered closed as if he hadn't heard a word she said.

Agnes whipped around to her mother. "Mama! Tell him. You can't want this for me."

But Mama looked like she wanted it very much. "He is handsome, Agnes. And strong. And he cooks. He plans to open a nice diner as soon as he saves some money and learns the language. He's smart, too. He'll make a good husband."

"For someone else." Her voice was low and harsh, almost drowned out by her chair scraping the linoleum as she stood. "Why?" she demanded. "You didn't arrange marriages for Irene or Helen. Why? Can't you trust me to find my own husband?"

Slowly, her father lifted his gaze to meet hers, any spark of joy gone from his eyes. "You are my youngest, and he is Greek, plus I am indebted to the Santorini family for a favor Allessandro has done. I do not have a son to marry his daughter, but he has a nephew, and you've been promised."

"*Promised?*" She choked on the word, backing away, looking from one to the other. "You can't do that to me!"

"Wait until you meet him, Agnes," her mother whispered. "He's very—"

"I don't care if he's goddamn Zeus!" she screamed, the exclamation like a shot that sent her father to his feet, knocking the table so hard his coffee spilled.

"You will not talk like that in this house!" he bellowed.

"No, I won't, you're right." Indignation bolted through her like a lightning strike. "I won't do *anything* in this house. Including live here. I'm leaving!" She ran from the room and ignored her mother's pleas to stop, her bare feet flying up the stairs two at a time.

They were serious! They were dead serious. Didn't they know that of all three Mastros daughters, she'd be the least interested in being manipulated like this? They knew she was strong-willed, independent, and...

In love with Norman Anderson. No, of course they didn't know that, but she was, and that was the only thing that mattered in the whole world.

She opened her tiny wardrobe and stared into it, her mind whirring. She'd run away, that's what. She'd run to Norman, and they'd elope. Tonight. Tomorrow. Soon.

Spurred by that thought, she reached under her bed for the tapestry bag she'd last used when she visited her aunt in Chicago, unclasping the strap to stuff clothes inside. She had no idea what she was packing, a dress, some skirts, some lingerie.

Lingerie that Norman would see if…

He'd wait until they eloped. Of course he would. He was a gentleman, and he'd wait.

She found a pair of leather shoes, brushed her hair, and put on some lipstick, then shoved her purse and some cosmetics into the bag, mentally calculating how much money she had. Enough to get her to the city, a little bit for food.

After that, Norman would take care of her. Wouldn't he? She kicked the uncomfortable thought away. Of course he would. He *loved* her.

She whipped around and stared at the oversize window, visualizing how she could climb down the fire escape. It would be tricky, but doable. And cold.

Her coat was downstairs by the front door. Damn it! Well, she'd have to freeze, then.

Grabbing the heaviest wool sweater she could find, she pulled it around her and buttoned it with shaking fingers.

Her mother hadn't followed her up here, thank God, but both her parents probably thought she was already lying on her bed, doodling "Mrs. Nikodemus Santorini" on a piece of paper.

Because they didn't know her at all.

But Norman did. And he loved her. He told her all the time that he loved her. When they fogged up the windows with hot kisses in his fancy company car, he said it over and over again.

With one last look in the mirror, she flung the bag over her shoulder and pushed the window all the way up to step out into the bitter air, her body quivering at the sudden cold.

"Agnes?" Her mother's voice outside the attic

bedroom door froze her more effectively than the air. She'd miss Mama. She really would. But not the ogre her mother was married to.

"Agnes, let me talk to you!" Mama called. "This boy is very handsome, Agnes. From a good family, and he'll learn English!"

She took one deep breath, grabbed the rail, and climbed down the icy metal stairs. There was only one boy for her, and by New Year's Day 1956, he'd be her husband.

Chapter Four

"**Y**ou ran away to marry a man named Norman Anderson?" Pru nearly choked on this revelation about Yiayia.

"On Christmas Day?" Gramma Finnie added, her own shock proof that her best friend had never shared this fun fact before.

"Quiet now," Yiayia said as they climbed the stairs to the front of the church. "We're in God's house."

"Where dogs are not usually welcome," Pru added, gesturing toward Gala and Pyggie. "One of us needs to stay out here with them. So I'll—"

"I'll stay with them," Yiayia said, taking Pyggie's leash from Pru. "You and Finnie go in and beg for the ticket."

Finnie and Pru shared another look of surprise.

"'Tisn't like you to give up control, Agnes."

She swallowed and looked up at the church. "I'd rather not go in, if you don't mind."

The way she said it sent a little chill through Pru, mostly because she hadn't ever heard a terribly contrite tone from this strong, highly controlling Greek woman.

"Of course, lass," Gramma said quickly, probably thinking the same thing. "This won't take but a moment."

"There's a coffee station over there on the grass," Pru said, pointing to some of the festival booth spillover and a large, enclosed tent. "They have plastic around the awning and warming lights, in case you and the dogs are chilly."

Yiayia nodded and took a step in that direction. "All right, then, go, you two," she ordered, sounding much more like herself. "Get that ticket." She glanced up at the church one more time. "I need that dog."

Without a word, Gramma Finnie and Pru headed up the last few stairs and opened the front door of the church. Although the large fellowship area was empty, they could hear voices, hammering, and some music coming from the massive sanctuary.

"You think she's okay?" Pru asked, pointing her thumb in the direction of the door behind them. "I'm surprised she'd give up the reins at a moment like this."

Gramma slowed her step. "She just confessed a sin, lass. Perhaps she's not ready to face our Lord yet."

Pru squished her face, still thinking of the story that couldn't have ended with her marrying Norman Anderson, or she'd be Agnes Anderson, not Agnes Santorini. "Running away from home isn't a sin, Gramma. She was eighteen, for one thing. And she didn't elope, but married a man named Santorini, just like her parents wanted her to. We know that much."

Gramma shook her head, silent. "Does not explain why she doesn't go to church."

"She doesn't go to church because she's Greek Orthodox, and the closest one is in Chestnut Creek, and she lives in Bitter Bark now." A tendril of frustration rose in Pru's chest, along with the need to defend the other woman. "Not to mention that it was pretty darn outrageous that her dad wanted her to marry some guy just because he was Greek and he owed a favor."

Gramma didn't say anything, but placed her hand on the large handle to open the door, her eyes fluttering shut as if she were praying, so Pru got a little closer.

"Gramma? You think she was wrong to run away that morning?"

"'Tis not my place to judge, lass."

"No kidding," Pru muttered as her grandmother opened the door.

Inside, the huge sanctuary of Bitter Bark's oldest and largest church was as decorated for the season as the square it faced. The altar area had been moved away for this event, with a professional-looking stage brought in and draped in red velvet curtains.

Those were open, and a full manger scene was visible, with a painted backdrop to look like the hills of Bethlehem, complete with a night sky and a bright star.

"Can I help you?" A woman approached with a clipboard and headset. "The church is closed right now, I'm afraid," she added.

"I'm looking for Melvin Jankewicz," Gramma Finnie said.

"Oh!" Her face brightened, and she looked at Gramma's arms. "Where's the baby?"

Gramma stared back and shrugged. "Not on me, lass."

"But you are bringing one?" The woman glanced at Pru. "We're good with Mary, but we need a baby Jesus. We thought someone might answer the emergency call we put out to all the churches."

Just then, a man marched across the stage and down the stairs on the right, and Gramma turned her attention to him. "Oh, there he is. Melvin?"

As she started to go, the woman put her hand on Gramma's arm to stop her. "Unless you have Jesus, I wouldn't bother him right now."

"I have Him in my heart," Gramma quipped, escaping the woman's touch to head to her target.

"I don't know what she wants from him," the woman said to Pru, "but this show has never been done without an actual baby, not a doll. The one we had came down with a cold, and his mother pulled him from the show. It's the worst possible moment to talk to Melvin."

Pru watched Gramma pad down the carpeted aisle, as determined in her own little Irish way as the much tougher Greek woman they'd left outside with the dogs.

"Melvin, I need to speak with you," Gramma said as she reached him.

Worried he might snap at her due to his stress, Pru followed, always ready to help her great-grandmother.

The man stopped midstep, scowling as he spoke into a headset, then the frown deepened. "No, you listen to *me*. It won't be the Christmas pageant without a real baby. There's never been a 'doll' used in Bitter Bark on Christmas Eve. It's a sacred tradition for the baby to be real. Even if it cries. Sweet baby Jesus, I need a sweet baby Jesus!"

"Melvin, a minute, please?" Gramma called.

"Finnie, I'm sorry, I know you need a Santa Claus, but I simply can't do it, and I don't know a soul who can help you."

"I don't need a Santa," she said, coming to a stop. "I need a ticket to tonight's show."

He snorted a laugh. "And I need a winning lottery ticket, which is about as likely as you getting in tonight."

"I'm sure you have one," she said. "And you offered a favor to me this morning."

He huffed out a sigh, pressing the headset to his ear. "I got show problems, Finnie. I have to go. Someone get me the reindeer guy on the line!"

He hustled away, and Gramma's tiny shoulders dropped in disappointment. And if she was disappointed, what would Yiayia be?

"I hear you need a baby," Pru called to him, the words out before she could take too much time and think this through.

Melvin jammed on his brakes and pivoted. "You have one?"

"As a matter of fact..." She threw a look at Gramma, whose blue eyes were wide behind her bifocals. "My baby brother is just four months old. He'd be perfect."

"Prudence!" Gramma whispered. "I very much doubt your mother would be pleased with that suggestion."

"Of course I'd have to stay with him and would be right behind the stage while he's out there," she added quickly. "And it's only one scene, right? At the end of the first act?"

Melvin came closer, his brown eyes pinned on her. "Yes, yes, and please, can I count on you for this baby?"

She slid a look to Gramma, lifting her brows in a silent communication the two of them had shared since Pru had been a baby.

"You may," Gramma Finnie said, crossing her arms like she did when she meant business. "For the small price of one ticket to tonight's show."

"Of course—"

"In the orchestra section."

His jaw dropped, then he laughed softly. "Okay," he said. "I'll get it for you when I have written permission from this child's mother that I can use this baby for one scene."

"Done and done," Pru said. "I'll go straight to my mom at her vet office and have her sign something. And then you have to give us that ticket."

"I will."

"You are making that promise in the eyes of God," Gramma reminded him, pointing to a stained-glass window.

"I give you—and Him—my word," Melvin said. "If you'll do the same and I know I have a baby for tonight's performance."

Gramma and Melvin shook on it, which Pru thought was amusing since they'd both made vows to God.

That settled, Pru hitched her arm through Gramma's and ushered her toward the back of the church. "Let's tell Yiayia the good news," she said.

"You think your mother will go for this?" Gramma asked as they left the sanctuary. "Or worse, your father?"

"I'll be with baby Danny the entire time," Pru assured her. "And we'll tell Dad these are heaven points. The man spent fourteen years in jail, remember? He's always joking about being out of God's good graces."

Gramma smiled at her as they stepped outside, the slate-gray clouds making it chillier and threatening more snow. "You were right, Prudence," she whispered.

"About the baby?"

"About me judging Agnes." She bit her lip and shook her head. "That was wrong, and we don't know the whole story, and I certainly did a few wild things in my youth."

"Like secretly meeting Seamus Kilcannon while you were working in a pillow embroidery factory," Pru teased, remembering Gramma's colorful and romantic history.

But Gramma didn't smile. "I wonder what else happened that Christmas Day."

"Think she'll tell us?" Pru elbowed Gramma playfully. "After all, I basically just sold my little brother into the church play so she can get her dog."

Gramma laughed as they got to the bottom of the steps. "Let's try and get it out of her, lass."

A few minutes later, they stepped into the oversize coffee tent, scanning the tables for Yiayia, who was in a spot near the back. As they walked closer, Pru's heart jumped when she saw Teagan sitting alone two tables away, staring at something on the ground near Yiayia, probably the two doxies.

"Oh," Pru whispered, slowing down a bit.

Gramma followed her gaze and put a gentle hand on Pru's back. "Just go talk to her and make things right."

But could things ever be right again after the way Teagan had treated her? She closed her eyes. "Okay. I'll try."

As they reached Yiayia's table, Pru saw that Teagan was watching her little sister, Avery, crouched down and playing with Pyggie and Gala, laughter like music coming from the little redhead every time one of them licked her face.

The minute Teagan saw Pru, she stood.

"Avery, we have to go."

Really, Teag? Why?

"'Tis fine," Gramma Finnie said to Teagan when Pru stayed silent. "Let the girl play. How are you, dear Teagan?"

Some color rose to her cheeks as she stole a look at Pru. "I'm good, but my, um, mom is probably finished with her shopping now, and my, uh, other friends are waiting. Let's go, Avery."

"No!" the little girl cried out, throwing her arms around Pyggie. "I love this dog. I *love* him!" Gala rose up and kissed the girl's face as if to remind her that she was lovable, too. "I love them both!"

With a tight smile, Teagan reached down and snagged Avery's jacket sleeve. "Up you go, schmoe."

Avery put up a fuss, but finally relinquished her hold on Pyggie and let Teagan walk her away.

"Bye, Teag," Pru said softly.

If she answered, Avery's protests drowned out the words. But Pru knew in her heart that Teagan had just walked away without even acknowledging her. The rejection stung and brought tears to her eyes, but Pru covered and sounded as bright as possible when she told Yiayia the news about the ticket.

Chapter Five

"Don't let it get to you, lass." Gramma Finnie put her arm around Pru a few minutes later as they headed to Mom's vet clinic off Ambrose Avenue.

"Easy for you to say," Pru mumbled, wrapping Gala's leash around her hand. "I didn't do anything to her, I swear."

"I told you," Yiayia said. "It's her, not you. Something has happened."

"Yeah, she turned horrible." Pru shook her head. "I don't want to think about her now. It's Christmas Eve, and we have to get that permission from Mom. That means we have to arrange to get baby Danny to the church, so we'll have to work around his feeding schedule, then get the ticket back to Rad Shepherd, then…"

"It'll be time to get ready to be Santa and Mrs. Claus," Gramma said with her singsong brogue full of joy.

"Oh, I almost forgot about that nightmare," Yiayia said under her breath.

"Agnes Santorini." Gramma shot her a look. "We

are spending half our day traipsing around this town for your dog. Having a happy attitude is the least you can do."

Yiayia looked a little sheepish. "You're right, Finola. I'm sorry."

At the rare softness in her voice, Pru leaned into her shoulder. "So, what happened, Yiayia?"

The older woman slid her a dark look. "You heard enough, missy."

"No, we didn't!" Pru exclaimed. "I'm dying to know what happened when you ran away on Christmas morning. I have to know. Did you get to Norman? Did your parents stop you? Did you—"

Yiayia cut her off with a wave of her hand. "I shouldn't have told you that much," she said. "I don't know what got into me. Christmas, I guess. Come on, Pru, we're here. Drop it."

Pru gave up—for the moment—lingering on the steps up to the red brick building where her mother worked when she wasn't the vet at Waterford Farm. Pru wanted to know the rest of Yiayia's story more than she wanted the dog-decorated leggings she'd put on her Christmas list, but she didn't want to push Yiayia.

Instead, she followed the others inside into Kilcannon Veterinarian Hospital, named after Grandpa Daniel, who'd opened it decades ago. Pru's mother, known locally as "Dr. Molly," was now the lead vet.

"No receptionist?" Yiayia asked, looking around the empty lobby.

"Mom probably sent her home early and stayed with the new kittens she delivered," Pru said, walking past them to the back offices she knew as well as any employee. She'd been raised in this building by a single mom who'd brought her to work nearly every day of her life. But Mom wasn't single anymore, since she'd married Pru's biological father last December and then little Danny was born, completing their family. "Mom? Where are you?" she called.

"Pru? Is that you? I'm in ICU."

ICU? That wasn't good. Pru picked up speed toward the last door in the hall, where only the sickest of animals ended up. "Are the kittens okay?" she asked, blinking at the long tabby on the table being given an IV.

"Perfect," Mom said, turning from the table to smile at Pru. "But their poor mama has developed eclampsia, and I need to give her a calcium cocktail for the next few hours."

"Ohhh." Pru went to the table to offer some love and sympathy. "What's her name?"

"Sprinkles," she said with a soft laugh, running her hand over the cat's head. "And she's sweet and only wants to nurse and love her little kitties." Mom leaned over, holding the IV line with one hand and dropping a kiss on the cat's striped head. "You will soon, my little darling."

Straightening, she looked up at the steady red light of a heart monitor. "I have to administer this very slowly and at very specific intervals, or her heart rate could drop. All done with the festival?"

The festival seemed like a hundred years ago. "Actually, I left right after I called you before."

"Oh, that's right. You need to grab Teagan's gift you left in the break room."

"I don't need it now." She sighed. "Long story that I'll tell you later. But I'm here with Gramma Finnie and Yiayia, and we're on a mission."

"Sounds intriguing." Mom laughed, then her smile faded. "Please nothing like last Christmas."

"We haven't even gotten in a car," Pru assured her. "But we are doing a bit of running around town for Yiayia." As Mom slowly adjusted the IV flow, Pru gave her a shorthand version of the story, pausing when she reached the big end. "So...I kinda promised this Melvin guy that Danny would be baby Jesus at the Christmas pageant this year."

Mom whipped around, her reddish-brown curls flipping over her shoulder. "You...what?"

"It's for a good cause, and honestly, it's a cool opportunity. Think of the pictures you'll have for his whole life!"

Her mother just stared at her.

"I won't let anyone else hold him. I'll stay with him every second—"

"Except when he's in a manger full of hay in front of hundreds of people."

"In the most coveted role in Bitter Bark. He's in one little scene, at the end of act one, and I'll zip him out of there the minute it's done. You can come."

She got a look that said this particular activity was not in the schedule. "Pru, it's Christmas Eve. I'm already committed to driving Gramma Finnie and Yiayia to Waterford Farm tonight after Gramma's done being Mrs. Claus."

"Perfect. Yiayia is Santa, and I'll be two seconds away at the church. The minute they're done with Danny, I'll wrap him up and bring him right to the square with them, and you can meet us there, and we'll all go to Waterford together. Good?"

"Not the Christmas Eve I envisioned, and I don't like him being on display like that."

"Well, Gramma Finnie promised God, so you better not bring His wrath on her."

Mom sighed and laughed at the same time and turned back to the cat on her table. "Well, I don't even know where Danny is right now."

"What? Doesn't Dad have him?"

"Trace had to help Garrett with a big rescue delivery. Six of the dogs that Alex and Grace brought in from that puppy mill in Winston-Salem have been adopted, and the families all asked for Christmas Eve delivery."

"Aww. That's wonderful."

"It is, but Katie had her hands full with party prep, so Trace dropped Danny off with your Uncle Liam and Aunt Andi, and they were taking the kids to Holly Hills for the elf parade and wanted to take Danny, too." She let out an exasperated breath like life was just a little too much today. "So, my four-month-old is somewhere in Holly Hills." Mom turned and narrowed her eyes. "Do not even *think* about going there."

Pru laughed. "Last Christmas scarred you, Mom. Don't worry. No wild rides to Holly Hills this year. So, when will they be back? Yiayia's getting antsy about this dog."

"Soon, I think. Why don't you and your granny friends go to lunch and wait?"

Pru felt a sad smile pull, knowing Mom was just being playful, but the truth hurt.

"What?" Mom asked, forgetting the cat to reach with a gloved hand for Pru. "Honey, what's the matter?"

"The grannies are my only friends." Pru shook her head. "That's all I have these days to lunch with."

"What are you talking about?"

"The reason I left the festival. Trouble with Teagan."

"Teagan?" She sounded shocked. "I adore that girl. She's so sweet."

"Not anymore. She ditched me for Sarah and Caitlin."

"Caitlin Phillips?" Mom made a face. "She doesn't have the best reputation."

"Right?" Relief that her mother so totally got it mixed with a new wave of distress over the situation. "Why would Teag prefer them to me? She absolutely ditched me."

"Oh, Pru. Girls your age can be rough," she said, stroking the cat with her gentle touch, but Pru knew that tenderness was directed to her, too. "Don't let it get to you on Christmas Eve. Go get a nice lunch, and when I have a minute, I'll call Andi and find out when they'll be back. If Danny's not too tired—"

"Too tired?" Yiayia's voice preceded her arrival in the doorway, with Gramma Finnie and the two dogs right behind. "You can't say no, Molly."

Mom smiled. "Well, I can, Yiayia, if my son isn't up to playing the part, but I know it's important to you, so we'll try to make it happen. I need a few more hours to get this new mama squared away and arrange for one of my vet techs to come in during the night, which won't be a fun call to make, and then we'll do what we—oh *shoot*! The ham!" Mom dropped her head back and grunted as if this one last thing had broken her. "I forgot the stinking ham."

"What ham?" Pru asked.

"I promised Dad and Katie I'd bring that really amazing sugar-glazed honey-something ham you can only get at Bitter Bark Butcher. Bob's holding one for me, but I know he's going to close early." She looked at Sprinkles. "Don't worry, I'm not leaving you, baby girl."

Pru's heart folded with affection for her mother and understanding that she was a little overwhelmed today. And, what was one more errand at this point?

"We'll get it," Pru said quickly. "We'll run over there right now, Mom. Don't even think about it."

Her mother's narrow shoulders dropped with relief. "Thanks, honey."

Yiayia came in to take a look at Sprinkles. "Will she live?"

"With my mom as the vet?" Pru gave Yiayia a playful poke. "She'll be fine. Now let's go get a ham." With a quick kiss on her mother's cheek, Pru ushered them all out of the ICU, down the hall, and back to the streets of Bitter Bark.

"You've quite the relationship with your mother," Yiayia mused as they stepped outside.

"Oh, those two lassies are two sweet peas in a pod."

Pru smiled at Gramma, but couldn't help noticing the sad look on Yiayia's face. "I know, you never had a daughter," she said, guessing that was why.

"But I had a mother," she replied.

48

"And the last we heard of her, she was telling you that the man your father arranged for you to marry was handsome but didn't speak English. Was she very mad at you for leaving that day?"

"That day? Oh, it was more complicated than just that day." Yiayia sighed and closed her eyes, slipping back to a different time and place.

Chapter Six

For Christmas Day, New York City was surprisingly empty. Agnes had expected the crowds she and her mother had met when they'd taken the Flushing Line from Astoria for their annual shopping day in the city.

Her boots crunched on soot-colored snow outside the 59th Street station, the sound and feeling pretty much what was going on in her chest at the thought of Mama. Would they ever have a shopping day like that again? Would her mother be proud to take Mrs. Norman Anderson to Carnegie Deli for pastrami sandwiches, laughing as they dug through their bags and relished the freedom of not eating Greek food for just one day? Forget the deli, would Agnes ever be welcome in her own home again?

She tamped down the fear and moved her bag from one hand to the other, looking up and down the nearly empty street to try to figure out where the Hotel Metropolitan was. That's where Norman said he was living while his company had him working the door-to-door sales job in the various boroughs of New York. She'd written it down when he told her, not long after they'd met about a month ago. And what a dreamy month it had been.

His company paid for a rent-a-car from Hertz, a red Ford Fairlane with white leather interior that squeaked against her skin when they made out in the back seat. Of course, she wouldn't let him come to the house in that attention-grabbing car, so she'd been telling Mama and Baba that she had a babysitting job. After dinner, he'd pick her up a few blocks away, near the florist on Ditmars Boulevard.

That was freedom and joy and excitement. They'd get a drink, find an empty parking lot, and talk and...

She shuddered despite a blast of hot air blowing up from a grate in the street.

They'd gone pretty far, that was true. Maybe a little too far, but no matter how much he begged and promised and kissed her until she literally couldn't breathe, she'd held him off and clung to the last shred of her virginity.

But now they could get married. He'd all but asked last time they were together, when he was trying so hard to slide her panties down.

I promise you, Aggie. We'll be together forever. Let me show you how much I love you.

She hoisted the bag over her shoulder and spied a policeman on the corner, walking his beat. Perfect. She could ask him where she could find the Hotel Metropolitan, which must be nice considering its fancy name.

"Excuse me, Officer?"

"Merry Christmas, young lady. Are you in from out of town?"

"Uh...yes. And I'm looking for my hotel. The Metropolitan? Can you tell me where it is?"

He gave her a sideways look, his frown deepening. "Why would you want to go there, if I may ask? Not exactly the best clientele in the city."

Oh, really? "I'm meeting...my husband," she said, loving the sound of the word on her lips. "His company sent him here on business, and I'm surprising him."

"He should think about a new company if they're putting him up at the Metropolitan," he said. "But you'll find it about six blocks that way and one block east."

"Thank you."

Seven blocks to get to Norman. Agnes practically pranced down the sidewalk, avoiding snowdrifts, smiling at the few people who were out on Christmas morning, her heart beating faster. Until she arrived. Then it just fell into her belly with a thud.

There wasn't a neon sign that faced the street, or a doorman, or...much of anything, just a few steps down into a street-level doorway that looked like it hadn't seen a coat of paint since 1937. The hand-painted words *Hotel Metropolitan* were the only way to confirm she had the right place, but the door was locked.

Darn! Did they close hotels on Christmas Day?

Frustration made her lift her fist and pound on the door, ready to fight for her right to see Norman.

After about ten noisy knocks, the latch flipped, and the door opened to reveal an older blond woman in a housecoat, who snuffed out a cigarette on the ground next to Agnes.

"Good Lord, even you girls have to take a break on Christmas Day. I ain't opening any rooms."

Agnes blinked at her. "I'm looking for Norman Anderson," she said. "He's a guest here."

The woman gave a soft snort. "Norm hasn't been here for a month or two, hun." She frowned a little, scrutinizing Agnes's features. "I don't remember you."

"I've never been here," she said. "But my… boyfriend stays here. He's a salesman."

"Oh, I know what he is. The guy with the brushes and the fancy red Ford. It gets him what he needs." She dropped her gaze over Agnes. "He's your… boyfriend? You sure about that?"

"Well, it's not…official, but I'm here to surprise him."

"Oh." She chuckled and pulled out a pack of cigarettes, lighting another one without taking her blue eyes off Agnes. "He'll be surprised, that's for sure."

Agnes stepped away from the puff of smoke, irritation and a little terror rising. "I need to find him."

Her gaze moved down to the tapestry bag. "You in trouble, hun?"

"Not…really. Nothing I didn't bring on myself."

"Mmm." She huffed out a smoky breath. "Ain't you cold?"

Freezing. "I'm fine. I just need to find Norman Anderson."

The woman thought about that for a long time, her brows knit together as she considered her response. Finally, she gave an exaggerated shrug. "Well, listen, when the men check in here, I make them give me a telephone exchange number. Want to call him?"

"If he's not here, then where would he answer the phone?"

"Beats me, but you can try. It probably rings to where he lives."

"He lives in hotels," she said, remembering the whole conversation. "He's a traveling salesman, and that's the life he lives."

"Well, you can try calling. You won't be any worse off if that number is as phony as the day is long. Some men are, you know."

But not all...*right*?

Pushing the door open, the woman gestured for Agnes to follow her into the tiny hallway that smelled like beer, cigarettes, and some really bad perfume she'd once bought at Woolworth's.

"What's your name, hun?" the woman asked.

"Agnes Mastros," she said without hesitation.

"Greek, are you?" She pushed open a wooden door with a number one on it and a sign that said Super nailed to it. The apartment was dimly lit and certainly did not live up to Mama's cleanliness standards. The place could have used a thorough dusting, and would it hurt to hang the clothes draped over the furniture?

"Thought you Greek girls stuck with your own kind," she said around the cigarette in her mouth, pulling what looked like a recipe box file from behind a toaster.

"We usually do," she said, knowing exactly what the woman meant. Her own kind would be Greek... like Nikodemus Santorini. "But not always."

"Not when they look like Norman," she said with a quick cackle. "And you, I gotta say. You're a pretty one. You two would make a nice..." She dropped her gaze to Agnes's stomach and stared. "Couple," she finished.

"We are," Agnes said, sounding as weak as she felt.

The woman clamped her lips around the cigarette and flipped open the box. Silently, she moved a few index cards, then took the cigarette out and smashed it into a small metal ashtray with the remnants of about ten others.

With each moment and movement, Agnes's stomach grew tighter. What tasted like her last bite of powdered sugar soured and made her tonsils swell like she might have to throw up right here on the faded rose carpet.

"I'm organized," the woman said, as if Agnes had accused her of not being so. "And I'm sure I have his…here it is. Norman Anderson, Fuller Brush. That him?"

She nodded. "That's…what he said." For some reason, everything he'd ever told her felt like it could go up in smoke as easily as this lady's Lucky Strike. Why would the Fuller Brush company make him stay here? They gave him that nice rental car.

"Here's a telephone number." She took a pencil and pad and wrote it down, saying the words as she wrote them. "Olympia 3-3937. There's a payphone in the Jewish deli down the street, and that'll be the only place open on Christmas. You'll need a dime. Got one, hun?"

She nodded, taking the piece of paper. "Thank you…ma'am."

The woman gave a yellowed smile. "It's Rita, and you're welcome. Happy I had the number. Just consider it your Christmas miracle. Good luck, hun."

"Thank you," she said again, folding the paper and shoving it into her pocket.

Outside, the freezing air stung her skin through the sweater and made her eyes water as she walked to the deli at the end of the street. At least she wished that was what made her eyes water. It couldn't be…regret. Fear. Disappointment. Or whatever that Rita woman planted in her heart.

Kaplan's was open and doing a surprisingly good business. On the wall just inside a chilly vestibule was a big black payphone that took Agnes's dime, gave her a tone, which hummed until her shaking fingers circled the dial seven loops, slowly.

A man picked up on the second ring, the sound of laughter in his hello.

"Norman?" she asked, hating that her voice cracked. She cleared it immediately. "Is Norman Anderson there, please?"

Dead silence. "Who is this?"

Only three words, but she recognized his voice, and relief washed over her. "Agnes. It's Agnes."

"How did you get this number?" he demanded, his voice low, hushed, and sickeningly harsh.

"I…" For some reason, she felt the need to protect Rita. "I just did. Don't you want me to call you?"

More silence and some shuffling. Then, "Agnes, what the hell? It's Christmas Day."

"I know, but…"

"Aren't you with your family?" he asked after a moment, his voice considerably softer and kinder now.

"I ran away," she said simply. "I want to…" *Marry you*. But something told her he'd hang up, and she'd never see him again. And she wanted to see him again. She had to. If not, she'd marry some Greek who didn't speak English and was going to own a diner.

"I want to see you," she finished, a little embarrassed at the seductive tone she used. But...she knew it would work. "I wanted to...be with you." She swallowed all the desperation that rose up like bile. She couldn't give up on him. Not yet. If they just saw each other... "You know how I feel, and...I want to show you."

She heard a soft intake of breath. "Later?" he said.

"Where are you? Where is this phone?"

Another beat of silence and shuffling. "My parents. In Brooklyn." It sounded like he was pressing the receiver against his lips. "I gotta just get through Christmas here, and then I'll make up some excuse..."

Make up some excuse? "Why don't you tell them you're seeing your girlfriend?"

"Because they're so old-fashioned, and they think I'm...single. They have weird ideas, you know?"

"Oh, I know." She actually smiled, happy they had parents with weird ideas in common. "How much later? I'm kind of stuck in the city at Kaplan's Deli, six blocks from the subway."

"Stay there as long as you can. I'll be fast. Don't leave, Aggie." His voice was low and warm. "I have a plan for us."

She clung to that plan, that warm voice, and that thin hope for four and a half hours in a booth at the back of Kaplan's. Fortunately, the waitress was nice and felt sorry for Agnes, who explained that her boyfriend was on his way, but stuck in a snowstorm.

So many lies, she thought as she sipped her fifth cup of coffee and checked the clock with dill pickle hands for the millionth time, staring at the words *It's always time for pickles!* in the middle of its face.

57

She tried not to think of what the Mastros Christmas Day must have been, forcing herself not to picture her mother crying and her father yelling and her two sisters furious that Agnes had spoiled the holiday.

Of course, they just thought she left in a huff over marrying some guy she'd never met. When they found out the truth…yeah, there'd be hell to pay, but…

She looked up as the door dinged and in walked the closest thing to a god that Agnes had ever laid eyes on. His short blond hair was shiny and combed so nicely, his face clean-shaven. His suit looked like he was about to start a day of knocking on doors to sell brushes and vacuums and anything else any poor housewife would buy just for the joy of looking at him for a few minutes longer.

He broke into a smile that revealed dimples and straight white movie-star teeth, holding her gaze as he slid into the booth across from her. He leaned forward, took her hand in his, and squeezed her fingers.

"Merry Christmas, gorgeous."

Just then, all was right with the world. "Merry Christmas, handsome."

He lifted her hand and pressed it to his lips. "We're going to Philadelphia."

She blinked at him. "Pardon?"

"My new sales gig starts the day after tomorrow in Philly. Come with me, sweetheart." He kissed her knuckles. "We can be there in a few hours, and Fuller already has a nice hotel."

Heat swirled through her, along with fear and anticipation and some kind of longing so strong, she didn't even know what to call it. She blinked at him, forcing herself to focus.

"If it's like the Metropolitan, I don't want to go."

"It's a Hilton. Top of the line. We'll stay there together."

"In the same room?" She felt all the blood drain from her face. "Without…getting married?"

He tipped his head as if to say, *Really, Aggie?* But he didn't say anything. He just kissed her hand again. "I'm working my way toward an assignment in Vegas. We can do it fast and sweet then. But for now…" He turned her hand and pressed his lips against her palm, his mouth searing her skin. "Be my girl, Aggie. Be mine. Tonight." He looked up through his thick lashes. "You know I love you."

Everything in her melted like the snow sliding in wet streaks down the window next to her.

"I love you, too, Norman."

He tugged her out of the booth, brushed his lips over her cheek, and whispered, "Let's go, Aggie."

For some reason she'd never understand, she couldn't say no to him.

Chapter Seven

"And?" Pru urged, frozen in her spot on Ambrose Avenue. "You went to Philadelphia with him?"

"Did you marry the lad?"

"What did your father do?"

"How did you end up as a Santorini, then?"

Pru and Gramma's questions fell as fast, but not as lightly, as the snow that had started as Yiayia finished her story.

"Where is this butcher shop?" she asked, looking around. "We've used them for meat supplies at my grandson's restaurant, but they deliver, so I have no clue where it is."

"You're avoiding the questions," Gramma Finnie said with a slight tease in her voice.

"Seriously, Yiayia," Pru added. "We have to hear the end."

"You've heard enough. You know...what I did. Now, let's get this ham and not freeze to death in the snow. Where to, ladies?"

"To Philadelphia," Gramma Finnie whispered. "Surely I didna know you had it in you, lass."

Yiayia gave her a sharp look. "You've never made a mistake, Finola Kilcannon?" Her voice was as sharp as Pru had ever heard.

"It's okay, it's okay." Pru put a hand on Yiayia's shoulder, surprised at how tense it was and that her body was trembling as it must have that winter day in New York when she made what had to be a pretty monumental decision in 1955. It would be monumental today, too. But then? To run off with a guy she barely knew? "It might have been a scandal back in the day, Yiayia," she said softly, "but no one is judging you today."

"No one?" Her dark gaze was pinned on Gramma. "Because I feel a tad bit judged."

"No, no," Gramma insisted, pulling her coat and scarf tighter. "The lass is right. I lived in those days, and I know that must have been a wee earth-shattering at the time, but I can tell you this, the Kilcannon women have quite the history of six-month pregnancies after marriage, if you know what I mean." She tried for a smile. "So no judgin' you for decisions you made in the, uh, bedroom."

Yiayia's eyes shuttered closed. "I can taste your judgment, Finnie. I can see the shock and disappointment in your eyes. I know what you're thinking. I'm as bad as the girls Rita took a cut from to use her rooms to rent by the hour at the 'Hotel Metropolitan.'" She made air quotes. "Took me a few years to figure it out, but boy, does it feel stupid to realize how naïve I was."

"Yiayia." Pru wrapped an arm around her. "You were naïve about a lot of things. You made a mistake a million girls have made. And Gramma's right. I come from such a long line of women who were pregnant when they got married that I'm afraid my father is going to chain me to the house when I'm eighteen."

Yiayia didn't smile at that, but she did shift her gaze away from Gramma. "Let's get the ham, for crying out loud. I want my dog." Her voice cracked. "I need my…Charis."

"Charis?" Pru asked, remembering she'd said it earlier. "What does that mean?"

"Never you mind, let's just get a move on." She ushered them all forward.

"All righty, then," Gramma agreed. "And let's hope this is the last stop before we can get the baby, get the ticket, get the dog, and get dressed as Santa and Mrs."

Yiayia just took a deep breath and exhaled as she walked, silent while Gramma prattled on about how Bob the butcher was the nicest man in Bitter Bark and treated his wife like a queen.

Pru stayed close to Yiayia, feeling the older woman's shame in telling her story and wanting to do anything to take that feeling away.

"Why do you want to name the dog Charis, Yiayia?" she asked softly. "Is that a Greek word?"

"Stop pestering, Pru! It's my dog to name how I see fit."

"Agnes." Gramma cooed her familiar reprimand when Yiayia used a particularly unpleasant tone. She did it frequently, Pru realized, and Yiayia never seemed to mind. She was usually grateful for the reminder.

But if the look she just gave Gramma was any indication, she wasn't grateful now. "Don't 'Agnes' me, Finola."

"All right, all right. I'm just trying to get you to calm down."

"I'm calm," she insisted. "Cold and tired and..." She closed her eyes. "Please, I'm begging you both. Don't ever share what I've told you. My son didn't know, so he never told Katie. No one knows. No one."

"Oh, Yiayia," Pru whispered, sliding her hand into the crook of the older woman's arm. "There's something special about friends who share secrets. That's what Teag..." She closed her mouth and bit back the rest. "Your secret is safe," she finished. "You have my word."

"And mine," Finnie added. "And an Irish woman's vow to secrecy is nothing to ever question, I assure you. Now turn here, and we'll be at Bob's in no time."

They walked in silence down the side street, noticing how many of the small stores had hung Closed signs for Christmas Eve. They'd taken a long time to get here, pausing to sit on a bench while Yiayia told her story. Maybe they'd taken too long.

They passed Bone Appetit, the dog treat store that Pru's cousin Ella ran, and Friends With Dogs, the grooming shop that her aunt Darcy owned. Both those were sealed up tight for the holiday. The last shop was Bob's, and Pru reached it first.

"Mom is not going to be happy," she said as she stared at the sign that said *Bitter Bark Butcher—Let Us Meat Your Needs*. And the one that said Closed below it.

"Oh dear," Finnie said when she caught up. "'Tis going to be a huge disappointment for Christmas Eve."

Pru waited for Yiayia to complain again, mad about the setback, focused on the dog, short-tempered with everything. But she shook her head, thinking.

"I had an issue with this butcher a while back," she said. "He made the wrong delivery to Santorini's during one of those weeks I was covering for Alex. It was long after hours when John discovered it, and he called, and Bob himself came in here, got our proper order, and delivered it to the restaurant that evening. If we call this shop, I believe the phone is forwarded to his home."

"Are you sure?" Pru asked. "Mom can live without the ham, and I don't think she'll renege on the offer to use Danny as baby Jesus, so we can still get the ticket."

But Yiayia already had her phone out, tapping the screen, then handing it to Pru. "I don't understand this Yelp thing, but there's the store number."

Pru took the phone, tapped the link, and listened to one ring.

"Bitter Bark Butcher! Happy holidays! How can we *meat* your needs?"

"Not sure you can, Mr...." She looked at Yiayia, who shrugged. "Mr. Bob."

"Let's try. Why are you calling?"

"This is Molly Bancroft's daughter."

"Oh goodness. Dr. Molly never got her ham," he said. "I went to her house, but no one was home."

He really did want to "meat" their needs, and that gave Pru hope. "She was called into the vet office, and my dad is out, but I'm standing in front of your store right now. Is there any way..." She let her voice rise and trail off.

"Oh, honey," he said. "I sold her ham to my last customer. I'd need to heat up the glaze now, and it takes a while to get right. And I would do it anyway for you, but..."

"We can wait, sir. And maybe we can help you with something?" What was one more errand at this point? Although it was getting darn cold for the dogs and grannies.

"I need to get a gift certificate from Bitter Bark Beauty for my wife's stocking, and I have to go right now. I'm afraid I did the manly thing and waited until the last minute."

Pru laughed, thinking of how most of her uncles were probably finishing their shopping this very minute.

"I'll get it for you," she offered without hesitation. "Can you let my great-grandmothers sit inside with their dogs while I run and get it?"

"I could do that, yes. I'm just two minutes away. Be right there."

"We can go with you," Yiayia said as Pru hung up.

"I think you should both stay here with the dogs, where it's warm, while he makes the ham glaze. I'll run over to the salon, easy-peasy."

"We can stay, Agnes." Gramma Finnie put her hand on Yiayia's arm, nothing but love in her eyes. "I'd like to chat a wee bit."

Yiayia just looked at her, silent.

"I've never seen you two genuinely mad at each other," Pru said. "If there's one thing I've learned today it's that friends are precious. You two need some time to talk. Take it."

"I should hope you've learned more than that,"

Yiayia said with a sniff. "Like how not to run away from home."

"I have to hear the end before I decide."

Just then, the lights inside the butcher shop came on, and the door opened from the inside. An older man Pru recognized beamed at them. "I know, I know, it's a Christmas miracle." He handed Pru a fifty-dollar bill. "One gift certificate from the beauty shop, please. They close in less than half an hour."

She took it and returned his smile. "I got this," she assured him, then put a hand on each of the older women's shoulders. "In you go, ladies. And don't come out without a glazed ham and a solid friendship."

Yiayia sighed, but Gramma patted Pru's cheek. "Yer a good one, lass."

Pru winked and took off for Bitter Bark Beauty, so invested in this darn dog that nothing would stop her from one last thing they needed to get it.

The problem was, Agnes didn't want to have a heart-to-heart with Finnie. She knew what the other woman must think of her, but her heart did feel just a little bit lighter having finally confessed her sin.

"Just have a seat, ladies," Bob said, rubbing a hand over his dome as he pointed to a tiny café table with two chairs next to the glass food display cabinet and the cash register counter. "I've got a little bit of work to do for Molly's ham, but it'll be ready in a bit. How about a nice bite of ham sampler for you two? And I can likely scare up some scraps for those dogs, okay?"

"Oh, that would be wonderful of you," Finnie said. "We've sure worked up their appetite today." When he disappeared into the back, Finnie dropped onto a chair with a sigh. "'Tis quite a kind thing he's doing."

"Oh, he's just trying not to lose customers. He knows my grandsons own a restaurant." Agnes took a load off, too, letting go of the leashes so Pyggie and Gala could sniff around, but both dogs merely curled up under a bench along the front window, as exhausted as the women were.

"A wee bit more walkin' than these old bones are used to," Finnie said, smiling at the dogs.

"You could go home at any time."

Finnie looked up, and the sadness in her eyes cut right through Agnes, and she knew what was coming. *Agnes! I thought you were tryin' not to be short with folks.*

"You really are angry with me," Finnie said. "I do so sincerely apologize for what I did."

Agnes closed her eyes. "Forget it."

"How can I when my nearest and dearest friend is hurtin'?"

"I'm not…" Oh, but she was. Agnes looked away, studying an ad on the wall for grass-fed beef, the words swimming before her eyes.

"You think I judged your actions, Agnes, and perhaps I did, but is my heartfelt apology not enough?" Finnie put a hand on Agnes's arm to get her attention. "Agnes?"

Cursing her tear ducts, she blinked. "Fine. Stop it, Finnie." She popped to her feet and walked a step away, staring into the back of the butcher shop. "What's taking him so long?"

"Agnes—"

"Don't *Agnes* me!" She whipped around, irritation heating her face. Irritation and…shame.

Didn't they just go hand in hand for her? Whenever shame burned, she lashed out at those closest.

And she was deeply ashamed right now. She felt shame because she'd done such a horrible deed as a young girl. And more shame because a woman like Finnie must think the worst of her. And even more shame because she swore that mean, nasty, short-tempered Agnes was gone…but here she was, back in full force. And Agnes *hated* her.

Finnie stood and took a step closer. "The memories are hurtin' you, lass."

"No," she whispered, her voice hoarse. "I'm just…rotten." And nothing would change that. She'd already been judged once by the only Judge who mattered. What made her think she could change and get another chance?

"You are not rotten." Finnie reached up and put her old knotted hands on Agnes's shoulders as Bob came out with some bowls for the pups, and after setting them down, he brought a small tray and put it on the table for them. "Won't be too long, ladies."

After he left, Finnie leaned in to whisper, "You are human. And when you think about something you did that was very, very human, you take all your self-loathing out on the people who love you the most."

Her shoulders sank under the weight of the words and Finnie's small but mighty hands. "You're so right, Finn." Tears welled.

The tiny woman pulled her close and patted her back with the tender touch of someone who'd soothed many, many loved ones in her life. "There, there, lass. 'Tis over. Whatever happened, you ended up with your sweet Nik. I know that much."

"But I carry this shame, Finnie. And it's what has made me such a nasty woman most of my life." Deep inside, she'd always known that. Always. But saying it made it so true and even more awful. She'd made her choice as an eighteen-year-old girl that Christmas afternoon. Maybe she hadn't really understood what she was getting into, but that was no excuse for what she did.

And the shame that hung over her for the next sixty-some years had turned Agnes into a shrew.

"You haven't been nasty for the part of your life that I've known you," Finnie said. "Granted, 'tis but a few months since you moved to Bitter Bark, but not only are you kind—most days—you've made an effort to soften your blows. Your whole family notices."

"I told you I was trying to improve for, you know, God." How else could she put it? "But then the real me comes out."

"The *old* you," Finnie corrected. "The real Agnes is standing in front of me, and I love her. And I do not judge her." She angled her head with her own embarrassed smile. "I admit I was shocked, but we're old ladies from another generation. 'Twas nothing, what you did." She added a smile. "Norman was that handsome, then?" She wiggled her brows. "What Cassie would call sex on a stick?"

But Agnes didn't laugh. She couldn't. "Oh, Finnie. It was so much…worse than what you think."

Finnie paled a little. "What happened?"

Agnes gave her head a sharp shake.

"You can't be free of it until you let it go, lass."

"I can't..." She closed her eyes, knowing that Finnie was right. With a quick glance to make sure Bob was still working in the back, she took a deep breath and guided Finnie to the table, where they sat, and each took a bite of the ham sampler.

"Philadelphia," she said when she swallowed, "wasn't quite what I expected..."

Chapter Eight

Agnes had never been so cold in her whole life.

It wasn't just the chilly hotel room, which, for a Hilton, wasn't ever warm enough. There was another kind of chill in this place...one in her heart. She'd lived in sin for a month, and the knowledge pressed on her chest every single morning, making her cold on the inside.

The bathroom door opened, and steam rolled out, warm and wet. And there stood Norman in his bathrobe, also warm and wet. He wiped a towel over his hair, which looked darker, setting off the blue of his eyes. Would she ever get tired of looking at a man as handsome as that movie star Tab Hunter?

Probably not. But she was damn tired of living in a hotel and waiting for him to say the words she wanted to hear and then act on them.

"Big day today, Aggie. I'm going to meet with my boss at corporate. Won't be home until late tomorrow night, if then. If that goes well, I'll be getting that mainline neighborhood next. Big money. Lots of vacuum cleaners for the fancy folks."

She barely heard a thing after *Won't be home...*

"It's not…home," she said.

"You having second thoughts, sweetheart?" He came right to the bed, where she shivered under a sheet, pulling it down to reveal her nightdress. He looked lustily through the thin material, his hand greedily covering her breast. "I can usually dispel those in a hurry."

He pinched her and moved in to kiss her lips, but she turned her face quickly.

"Hey, hey, Aggie. None of that when I want to kiss you."

"I haven't brushed my teeth yet."

"As if I give a damn about your teeth." He lowered his head and began kissing the bare skin of her décolletage, his tongue like sparks on her skin. Instantly, she responded, but before she let her stupid body take over, she squeezed her eyes shut and inched him away.

"Norman, how much longer?"

He lifted his head, cleared his focus, and eased back. "A little while, baby."

"What does that mean?"

"It means there's a hierarchy to my business, and I can't just demand time off."

"You had two days last week and left me here."

His eyes flashed. "Sales meetings at headquarters," he ground out, because he was obviously sick of telling her this. "You don't make President's Club if you skip the corporate rigmarole. You know I'm on a ladder, and a man's gotta climb it without…" He gave her a warning look that she absolutely hated. "*Demands*."

Her stomach burned as she sat up a little straighter. "You promised."

"I *discussed possibilities*."

"You promised Las Vegas," she shot back, refusing to be daunted by his arguments.

"Because I thought I might be able to work out there, but there aren't enough neighborhoods to sell household products in the middle of the desert. Just some gambling halls."

"And a place called A Little White Wedding Chapel," she whispered. "I was in the market and read last week's *Time* magazine, and there was an article about it. You can get married in a matter of hours."

He stared at her, silent. It might have been the first time she'd used the word *married*, but surely he knew what she wanted after all these weeks.

He didn't say a word.

"Norman, you said you wanted...this...to be permanent." Did she have to be the one to ask? Did he want her to do that? Because, she would.

"It is permanent. We're here, in Philly...sharing our lives. I could have this territory for a while, and this isn't such a hellhole to live in on the company dime. Except for the heat problem, it's a good life."

"Norman, I don't *have* a life. I'm in this hotel room, waiting for you all day and half the night."

"But when I come home..." He reached for her breast again, but she swiped his hand away, making his eyes glint in anger. "Look, Agnes, I told you to get a part-time job. It wouldn't bother me if you had a job."

"I don't want a job! I want a husband!"

He flinched a little, as if she'd slapped his face. Then he swallowed and slid off the bed, untying his robe. Dead silent, he opened the closet door and disrobed in front of her. Agnes's cheeks warmed. She was still not used to the sight of a naked man, no matter how many times she'd shared his bed.

"I'll leave you a little cash," he said with aching nonchalance. "So you can eat something, maybe take in a movie."

Cash. It made her feel like…the way that lady at the Hotel Metropolitan had looked at her. An ugly, sinful word she'd never used burned in her head.

Whore.

But what could she do? She'd sent a letter to her family and told them she'd left with her boyfriend and was marrying him, reminding them that she was eighteen years old and able to do whatever she wanted with her life.

Including *ruin* it.

Silent, she watched him put on his shirt, knot his tie, splash on some cologne, and take that money out of his wallet. Without a word, he set it on the corner of the dresser.

She stayed in bed, giving him a perfunctory kiss when he left, closing her eyes for a good ten minutes. When she opened them, his few dollar bills were the first thing she saw.

No. That was not who Agnes Mastros was.

Throwing back the covers, she got up, put on the only nice dress she'd brought, brushed her hair, added some lipstick, and got her handbag. She'd try the little market down the street, the bakery, maybe that breakfast diner. She'd get a job and a way to pay for her own damn food and movies.

She heard raised voices as she walked toward the tiny lobby, making her slow her step.

"How can I get the rooms cleaned by check-in time, Mr. Horowitz? There's only two maids, and Vera is, you know, in the family way. What will guests think of that?"

"I'll terminate her tonight, Bill," another man said. "We can't have a woman looking like that cleaning the rooms. Let me run an ad, and we'll replace her."

Replace her? She sailed around the corner and walked up to the two men deep in discussion, recognizing one as the manager, but not the other, a more distinguished man deep into his fifties.

"I would like to apply for that job."

The older man drew back in surprise, but the manager eyed her closely. "Aren't you and your husband in room thirteen?" he asked.

"We are," she replied without missing a beat at *husband*. "But he's on the road so much, and frankly, I miss housekeeping." She smiled from one to the other. "I was trained by the best, in New York City."

At their skeptical looks, she squared her shoulders and looked Bill the manager right in the eyes. "And I can start today. All I need is a uniform and some supplies."

The manager gave a pleading look to his boss, who nodded. "Problem solved," he said. "What's your name?"

"Agnes Ma... Anderson. My name is Agnes Anderson." And maybe it would be someday, but until then, she would not get paid by her...lover.

"Come on, Agnes. I'll get you a few uniforms to try on, and then you can start with your own room, and I'll see how it looks when you're done. If it passes muster, you have a job."

"Terrific."

Not an hour later, wearing a navy uniform dress with the words *Hilton Maid* embroidered on it, Agnes knelt before the toilet with a scrub brush, using as much elbow grease as the cleaner in her bucket. The cleaning solution was cheap, though, and didn't work. She'd have to ask Norman to give her some of his latest—

The hard knock on the door brought her head up sharply. Bill—er, Mr. Dunn—already? She wasn't ready for the inspection. She hadn't finished the bathroom or even made the bed. As she sailed past the messy sheets, she grabbed her nightshirt and slippers, looking around for any other personal items of hers, and stuffed them into the top dresser drawer.

"Norman, are you in there?"

The woman's voice brought Agnes to a freezing halt. Who was that? She stared at the door, speechless.

"Norman!" The woman laughed. "You said you were taking today off. And I drove all the way from Brooklyn to surprise you, honey."

Honey?

Suddenly cold all the way to her veins, Agnes walked to the door like she was striding through mud, opening it with one hand, the toilet brush still in the other.

A young brunette with beehive hair and bright red lips stood at the door. "Oh," she exclaimed, then her gaze dropped to Agnes's chest. "Oh, you're the maid. Did Norm…uh, Mr. Anderson step out while you clean?"

Who was this? "He went to work," Agnes said.

"Oh, he did, huh?" The woman sailed in, right past

Agnes, shaking her head. "Or did he drive to New York to surprise me?" She turned, laughing. "Wouldn't that be something? Like that short story about the couple who buy each other Christmas presents but have to sell the things…" She waved her hand. "Never mind. You wouldn't know."

The Gift of the Magi. Of course she knew.

"But it *would* be pretty hilarious if we both had the same idea for a surprise on our anniversary."

"Anniversary?" The word caught in Agnes's throat.

"Three years married," she said in a singsong voice. "I'm Gloria Anderson, by the way. The wife of the man staying here." She glanced around the room. "And I see he's still not neat when I'm not around."

Agnes couldn't move. She couldn't breathe or think or speak, either.

Gloria Anderson had no such problem, humming as she walked to the dresser to look at herself in the mirror, patting her hair, then she pointed to the money, a diamond flashing on her hand. "My, he's a good tipper for the help, though."

Heat roiled through her. "Yes," she said through gritted teeth. "He's been very…generous."

The woman turned and eyed her sharply, her gaze once again sliding over the maid's uniform. "Well, I'll just go wait downstairs. I'm sure he'll be back soon."

Agnes just nodded, standing stone-still with her broken heart and toilet brush.

As soon as Gloria Anderson's footsteps faded, she packed her bags and left through the back door of the hotel, not even bothering to take off the uniform.

Her only consolation was that the money was still on the dresser.

Chapter Nine

Holding the gift certificate carefully so it didn't get bent, Pru marched through the streets of Bitter Bark at a much faster clip than she had with two octogenarians and a couple of dogs all day. Still, she had to admit, the adventure had been fun.

But it was late in the afternoon, and this had to be the very last errand before they could get Yiayia's dog.

She pushed open the door of the butcher shop just as Bob emerged from the back, holding his prized ham. "Here you go, ladies. Christmas glazed ham for the big Kilcannon and Mahoney..." He smiled at Yiayia, who, along with Gramma Finnie, pushed up to a stand. "And *Santorini* feast tonight. Merry, merry Christmas to all at Waterford Farm."

Both women were a little flushed, Pru noticed, and Gramma's eyes looked as glazed as the ham. Had she been crying? Had these two old besties had a fight like Pru and Teagan? She felt her heart drop at the thought, anxious to make them laugh again.

She waved the envelope at the butcher. "And you can stuff your wife's stocking tonight, Bob!"

Yiayia and Gramma looked at each other and snickered, thank goodness, so Pru gave Yiayia's arm a playful jab. "Clean up your minds, you two."

Bob cracked up, too, though he'd turned the same color as his holiday ham, all the way up to his bald crown. With some hugs and more holiday good wishes, the three of them stepped out to the sidewalk, noticing the sky had grown dark with even more snow threatening, and the temperature had dropped.

"Goodness, it's getting late," Gramma said, looking at her watch. "We only have about an hour and a half until we have to be dressed in our costumes and in place at the festival."

"We can make it," Pru said, getting behind them and putting a hand on their backs with the tiniest amount of pressure. "First, we take the ham to Mom, then we take her signed permission slip to Melvin at church, then we take the ticket he gives us to Rad, get our dachshund, and we're done! After that, I'll snag baby Danny, assuming he's at Uncle Liam's house by now, and take him to church for the play, and you two dress up and head to the square. Sound like a plan?"

In front of her, the two women shared a quick look and silently communicated something Pru could not begin to understand.

"You two are okay, right?" she asked, a tendril of worry curling through her. "Because I can take a lot of things today, but not a tiff between my favorite two grannies in the world."

"We're fine, lass." Gramma reached back and put her hand on Pru's shoulder, inching her forward so she could walk between them. "We had a good talk and figured out all the things in life."

Pru sighed with relief. "Like what? My things in life could use some figuring out."

"Sorry, Pru," Yiayia said quickly. "What we discussed is between your great-grandmother and me."

"Did I miss more of your story?"

They shared another look, then Gramma shook her head. "Not a bit," she said. "We just rested our weary bones in there. Was Danielle working at the salon? She does such a nice job with my hair."

Pru recognized a subject change when she heard one. And what her little Irish grandmother called a *whitie*—a small lie meant to protect a loved one. So she backed off, because whatever had happened when Yiayia ran away, it was clear that telling Gramma more of the story had upset her.

"Danielle was out, and they were closing. Looks like all Bitter Bark businesses are shutting down early for Christmas Eve," Pru noted as they turned the corner to Mom's office.

Yiayia threw her a look, her eyes soft. "You're a good girl, Prudence," she said softly.

Pru smiled. "Thanks, Yiayia. Did you ever notice that when you want someone to know how much you love them, or you really want to drive home a point, you use their full name?"

"Do I?"

"Yup." Pru nodded. "You call Cassie 'Cassandra' and Alex 'Alexander' and John 'Yianni' with that pretty Greek accent."

Yiayia tipped her head. "I do that? I never realized it."

"And then you want to make food for them," she added. "You love in your own special way, Yiayia. It's very nice."

The older woman blinked, obviously fighting a tear. "Why, Prudence, that's the sweetest thing anyone has said to me since..." She glanced at Gramma and gave a soft laugh. "Well, since ten minutes ago when your grandmother wrapped me up in her own kind of love."

Pru grinned at them, fully relieved that they'd made up. "Well, if you have any advice for how I can wrap up my ex-hopefully-not-forever best friend next time I see her, let me in on the secret."

As they reached the vet office, Mom opened the door, her arms outstretched...for the ham.

"You got it!" she exclaimed.

"We sure did," Pru said, planting a kiss on her mother's cheek as she handed her the precious ham. "Did you sign a permission slip for the church to use baby Danny during the manger scene tonight?"

"I did." She waved them into the front office and grabbed a piece of paper from the reception desk. "My vet tech is running late, and I just can't leave Sprinkles yet. But Liam and Andi are home, and the baby had a huge nap in the car, so hopefully he won't be a cranky Jesus."

"That's great," Pru said. "But are you going to make it to Christmas Eve dinner, gifts, and Midnight Mass?"

"Midnight Mass might be a stretch with a four-month-old, but I doubt any of the babies will be going this year. I'll make the rest. Remember, you are in charge of your brother at that church, Pru," she added with a quick point of her finger. "I expect him to be treated like he really is the Savior of the world."

"I planned on it, Mom, and I promise you I'll never

let him out of my sight, and the minute the end of act one curtain comes down on the shepherds, I'll get him out of there. Will you still be here?"

"I should be, but I hope Cara Lee will arrive by seven, at the latest."

"That's when we'll be done playing Santa and Mrs. Claus," Gramma said.

"Santa?" Mom looked at Yiayia. "You?"

"It's my own personal Christmas miracle."

Mom snorted a laugh. "Well, then I'll have Trace take this ham to Waterford early, and I'll drive you three, the baby, and the dogs to Waterford." She blew out an exaggerated sigh. "It all works out."

"Except there will be three dogs, Molly." Yiayia gave a big smile. "We're going to get my newest right after we drop this paper off at the church."

Mom laughed. "We can handle three dogs. Off you go, I have to check on Sprinkles."

With another quick kiss, they said goodbye and headed straight to First Baptist of Bitter Bark.

This close to the performance, the church was much busier than it had been a few hours ago. Actors in costumes and makeup, no doubt from a dress rehearsal, bustled around. Mary and an angel sipped coffee on a bench in the entryway, while King Herod paced and recited his lines. Some of the choir, in long red robes, huddled together, warming up, and a couple of wisemen sat in the back row of the sanctuary, playing cards.

"Have you seen Melvin Jankewicz?" Pru asked one of them as their eyes adjusted to the dim light.

"Backstage," one said, pointing. "Go at your own risk. He's so worried about not having a real baby

Jesus that he's probably said a few words never uttered in this place before."

"Oh, I bet they've been uttered," Gramma said in a stage whisper, cracking them all up.

"He'll be singing praise music soon," Pru assured them, waving her permission slip. "I have his baby."

The wisemen let out a soft cheer as the three of them headed toward the stage and followed the booming voice of the set director until they found him. His eyes lit at the sight of them.

"Please tell my you've got a baby."

"Here's my mother's permission slip. I'll go get him right now and bring him over..." She paused for effect and let Yiayia finish.

"For a ticket, sir."

"Absolutely!" He reached into his pocket and plucked out his wallet, extracting a ticket. "Second row, middle of the stage."

They all cheered, hugged, and headed out, waving the ticket in victory as they left.

"You can go get Danny, lass," Gramma said. "We'll take the ticket to Rad Shepherd."

"I have time to go with you," Pru said. "After all this, do you think I'm going to miss the moment Yiayia wraps her arms around her new baby and pronounces him Charis? Maybe she'll even tell us why."

Yiayia pointedly ignored that suggestion and hustled them all toward Rad's house, the three of them walking as fast as possible, considering the snow had started to fall again. The dogs weren't fazed, though, trotting with purpose after their short rest and delicious snack at Bob's. And they seemed to pick up the fact that something exciting was about to happen.

They turned the corner on Rad's street, admiring some Christmas lights that were coming on with the dimming late afternoon light. The snow danced around them and the lights as the dogs led them.

"They're like our own little reindeers," Pru joked.

"Dachshund through the snow," Gramma sang out, making them all laugh.

"On a two-dog open sleigh," Yiayia added to the tune.

"Over roads we go, laughing all the way!" With howls and hoots and tingly holiday joy, they sang their version of "Jingle Bells" all the way down the street, arm in arm, as happy as Pru had felt all day.

They finished with a flourish as they reached Rad's front door, ringing the bell and giggling like three little kids.

But this time…no sweet dog barked at the sound of the doorbell. In fact, they stood for a good thirty seconds of silence before the first wisp of worry wended its way through Pru.

"Maybe he's in the back," she suggested.

"Or taking the dog for a wee bit of air," Gramma added.

But Yiayia's face hardened, and her eyes narrowed, and her jaw set in that way Pru just knew preceded something cold and nasty. "Maybe he just blew us off."

"Why would he do that, Agnes?"

"Who knows why men do anything? They can't be trusted." She breathed so hard, a puff of white air surrounded her nostrils. "I should have known."

"Agnes, please. We don't—"

Just then, a car pulled into the driveway, and all three of them turned with hope and relief.

Rad opened the driver's door and scowled, his frown a mix of disbelief and concern.

"Uh, you came back?"

"Of course we came back." Yiayia's voice rose. "With the ticket. Where's my dog?"

He huffed softly and closed the car door, walking closer. "I sold him, ma'am."

"*What?*" That came from all three of them, followed by Pyggie's loud bark.

"I'm sorry...I..." He reached them and looked sheepishly from one to the other. "When you didn't come back, I figured you didn't get a ticket. This nice young couple stopped me in the square and started asking about him, and it turned out the guy had just been given a ticket he couldn't use and..." His voice trailed off as all of them—including the dogs—stared at him.

"Well, I guess you can play Judas in the Easter play," Yiayia snapped, stepping away.

"Agnes," Gramma whispered, but her familiar warning held little bite.

"Hey, I'm sorry. That dog damn near ate Ralphie. I had to get rid of him, and you guys took forever. You'll find another dog, I'm sure."

"I'm sure we will," Gramma said, walking after Yiayia to console her.

"Did you get the name of the couple who got the dog?" Pru asked with one last desperate shred of hope.

He shrugged. "I didn't even ask, sorry."

On a sigh when she realized the adventure had ended, Pru said goodbye and tugged the leashes to catch up with Gramma and Yiayia.

"I'm so sorry, Yiayia."

She just shook her head, silent.

"There will be other dogs," Gramma Finnie said. "Garrett is still looking for that perfect doxie for you, and if anyone can find a dog, it's my grandson."

She sniffed, obviously fighting tears. "It wasn't meant to be," she said. "My Charis...I'll never get it because I don't deserve it."

It? Why would she call a dog *it*?

"Hush, Agnes." Gramma Finnie put her arm around her. "You go on to Liam's, lass," she said to Pru. "Dog or no dog, you've committed to bring baby Jesus. Agnes and I will go get dressed, and I'm sure handing out some gifts to children will take her mind off the blues."

Yiayia sighed, her disappointment palpable. Pru didn't understand why this dog mattered so very much, but her heart broke for the old lady who certainly wasn't getting what she wanted for Christmas.

She stood in the snow and watched them walk away, their heads close.

"Thanks for not telling Pru what I shared at the butcher shop," she heard Yiayia say.

"'Tis nothin' she needs to know, my friend. But I need to know the rest, and right this very minute, too."

Pru's jaw dropped as their voices faded when they turned the corner. As much as she wanted to run after them and demand to hear the story, she knew some secrets were supposed to be between best friends.

If only she had one.

Chapter Ten

No journey had ever seemed so long, exhausting, or painful as the one from Philadelphia to Astoria. The buses were filthy and sour-smelling, the subway broke down twice, and when Agnes finally got to Ditmars Boulevard, she simply didn't have the strength to walk the last few blocks in the pouring rain. She never did get a proper coat—another thing Norman had promised, but didn't deliver—so she stood under the overhang of Astoria Florist in the very spot where she used to wait for him to pick her up in his big red Fairlane.

Was he driving his wife in it now?

A fresh onslaught of tears threatened as a gray panel truck with the florist logo on the side pulled up fast enough to send a rooster tail of rainwater from the gutter all over her once-crisp navy maid's uniform.

Instantly, the truck pulled over, and the driver jumped out.

"Sorry!" he called. "I am so sorry, miss." The rolled R of a Greek accent was common enough in Astoria, which had the largest Greek population in all of New York, but this man was anything but common. Tall and dark with narrow but sturdy-looking shoulders, he strode toward her with no regard for the rain and only concern on his handsome features. "My…not good. My not good."

She managed a smile. "It's fine," she said. "Worse things have happened to me today."

"Inside?" He pointed to the door. "So you no get…" He turned that finger toward the open skies. "Sat…satur…"

"Saturated," she supplied, her gaze dropping to the badge pinned to his uniform shirt. Nik. The most common of all Greek names, but not with that spelling. "I don't want to go inside. I'm not buying anything. I'm…waiting for…" *The nerve to face a family who hates me.* "Someone."

"You no buy," he said, pulling the door open. "I work. You dry."

She searched his face—his kind eyes, and sweet smile and guileless warmth—and fought another sob. Why couldn't she have fallen for him instead of—

"Come," he said. "Inside."

"Okay," she agreed, stepping into the tiny storefront, instantly surrounded by the rich scent of roses and lilies and freshly cut greens. "Thank you."

"*Tipota.*" He gave his head a quick, hard shake. "I mean…you are…"

"Welcome," she said, squeezing some water from her hair. "Recent arrival?"

He frowned and shook his head.

"Did you just get here?" she asked, enunciating each word.

"One month," he said. "From Santorini."

88

It took a second, but then the name hit her heart. *Nik.* From *Santorini.*

Oh God, could You be any more cruel to me today? "That's nice," she muttered.

He pointed to the back. "I go make the flowers." He bunched his hands together to indicate a bouquet. "You wait or…come?"

She just stared at him, hearing her mother's words. *He's very handsome, Agnes.*

That was an understatement. And Mama forgot to mention he was sweet and…kind. "I should…go."

"You wait for someone." He pointed to the window that divided the front desk from a florist workspace in the back. "We see your someone. You go then. Now, help me." He angled his head and gave a smile that slid through her heart and curled her toes. "I am not good at the…boo…"

"Bouquets."

He laughed. "I should know bouquets."

"It's all right," she said. "It's French, not English." On a sigh that communicated just how much she regretted every decision she'd made in the last month, she followed him through the swinging door to a small room with a refrigerated wall full of fresh-cut flowers. He got her a small stool and a dry towel and set her up so she could look straight through the front glass of the store to see someone…who didn't exist.

She perched there and watched him take a piece of paper from a pile and frown, reading it. "Today I make the flowers *and* deliver," he said. "I am promo…higher up."

She smiled. "And you've only worked here a month?"

He gave her a sideways look from his worktable. "I work hard."

"I bet you do." A hard worker, a good provider, and no doubt he'd be faithful, too. Oh, sad lessons learned.

And soon, when the word got out that she was back, maybe he'd come to meet Agnes Mastros, and he'd need to know the truth about her. Then he could have his uncle find another, more pure and innocent Greek girl to be his wife in his new country.

There was really only one thing to do.

"My name is Agnes," she said softly.

"Good Greek name."

"Agnes Mastros."

His hand froze in the act of putting a red rose in a vase. "Oh." He inched back and blinked at her, then something crossed his face she couldn't quite read. Surprise, then disappointment, maybe. She was about to make that worse. "You've been…gone."

"I have been. You're Nikodemus, aren't you?"

He nodded, still scrutinizing her, nodding slowly. "I saw your picture, but not…the same. You are different."

She sure was. "Did they tell you anything?"

"That you are pretty." He tipped his head, the slightest smile pulling. "They not tell truth."

Her eyes widened.

"You are…*omorfi*."

Beautiful.

She felt a flush warm her cheeks. "Not really," she said, looking down. "I am…" Spoiled. Used. Damaged. "Not good for you."

His laugh brought her gaze back to him. "I will decide that."

His optimism was sweet, but she wasn't going to take advantage of him, only to let his heart be smashed when the truth came out. And it always came out, as she'd learned today.

"Nik, I...I don't know where my family told you I was for the past month, but you should know the facts." At his puzzled look, she added, "The truth? The honest truth?"

He nodded, silent for a long moment. "We were betrothed," he finally said. "That is the truth."

She swallowed hard. "In this country, in this day and age, that is debatable." She knew he didn't have any idea what that meant. "We can only be betrothed if we both agree."

He nodded quickly. "I agree."

Oh sweet Lord, could he be any better? "But I..." *Should have agreed.* Sight unseen. No questions asked. This man would make someone very, very happy. "I was in love with another man."

She waited until his brain translated that. "Love?" he asked. "Another?"

"Yes. I went with him. Far away. For the past month."

A little blood left his cheeks. "Is that who you wait for?"

"No," she whispered. "He betrayed me."

"Be...tray?"

"He cheated."

He shook his head, still not getting it.

"He was married." She held up her left hand and squeezed her ring finger. "To another woman."

His eyes widened as comprehension dawned. "He should die."

For some reason, that made her laugh. "Yes, he should."

"Why he do that to you?" He closed his large hand around a rose stem, cracking it.

"'Why was I so stupid?' is probably a better question."

He put down the broken flower and turned to her, taking a step closer. "You did not want me."

"I didn't know you," she said softly. "And I...I thought..." Her voice cracked as the pressure of the day, the month, and a mountain of regret hammered her down. "I thought I knew what I wanted, but..." A sob escaped. "I was wrong. So wrong."

He stared at her, silent, judging, no doubt, and counting his blessings for narrowly escaping a life with a woman as scorned and scarred as Agnes Mastros. He looked hard with his near-black eyes, so dark she could see her own reflection in them.

His square jaw was set with anger and what she assumed was disgust as he had to realize what she'd been doing with a married man for a month. A vein in his neck pulsed, his chest rose and fell, and finally he looked down to the ground.

"I'm so sorry," she rasped.

Before he could say another word, she shot off the stool, grabbed her bag, and launched out the swinging door, marching right into the rain to let it wash away her tears.

She'd done her duty and told him the truth. Nikodemus Santorini was off the hook. Now she had to face her family.

Oddly buoyed by the exchange she'd just had, Agnes headed home to the three-story brick house just off Crescent Street, not bothering to knock before she opened the door.

Mama was in the kitchen, visible from the door, and Baba sat in his big chair in the parlor, reading a newspaper, which he lowered to reveal a silent, furious, shocked expression.

"I'm...home," she said.

"Agnes!" Her mother flew out from the kitchen, a wooden spoon still in her hand. "Agnes, you're—"

Agnes held up her hand to stop her hug, not wanting her sweet mother to touch her wretched daughter. "Please. I have to...I have to tell you what happened."

"We *know* what happened." Her father slammed down the newspaper with a scary amount of force.

"Are you married?" Mama's voice rose in fear, as if she already knew the answer.

"I am not."

"You ruined yourself and this family!" her father exclaimed, agony in every word.

She turned and met his gaze. "I did. I don't suppose saying I'm sorry will change anything."

"You're not welcome in this home. Get out."

Even though she fully expected this, Agnes sank with the blow.

"Wait, Estevan," her mother said. "Let her talk. She hasn't told us anything."

"She wrote it all down. She gave herself to a man outside of marriage." He ground out the words as if they hurt coming out of his mouth. "Like a..." He rooted for the word, which they all knew, but even he couldn't utter it.

"He was married," she whispered.

Her announcement was met with dead, shocked silence.

"I left when I found out." Not that leaving saved her from the enormous shame she could feel filling the entire house. Nothing could save her from that.

"You will leave," her father said, much quieter now, no doubt rocked by this new blow.

"I will," she agreed.

Her mother let out a soft sob.

"I'm sorry," she said and finally put her hand on Mama's shoulder. "I don't expect you to forgive me. I don't expect...anything."

"What will you do?" Mama asked on a ragged sigh.

Agnes answered with a tight smile, tapping the hotel logo on her chest. "Work. I have some experience as a maid." With that, she hoisted her bag and headed for the stairs to her room. Surely they'd let her change and get more clothes.

No one followed, but she heard her parents' harsh whispers in her wake.

Her room looked the same, smelled like her favorite cologne, her bed neatly made. She sat on the edge of it for a moment, waiting for tears that didn't come.

She changed her wet clothes, brushed out her hair, and opened the dresser drawers and packed, much slower this time, moving like her body was in a bowl of molasses, heavy and nearly paralyzed.

When she'd repacked her suitcase and hoisted it over her shoulder again, she took one more look around, pausing to decide what else she'd like to bring from home. A small painting of St. Agnes that her yiayia had given her for her twelfth birthday? The patron saint of girls and chastity? She almost laughed at the rich irony there.

There was a doll her mother had made her perched on a shelf, a necklace her father had given her for her eighteenth birthday hanging on a hook, a tattered copy of *Five Little Peppers and How They Grew*, her favorite novel as a young girl.

But that girl was gone forever, taken by Norman Anderson and never to—

She heard the sound of a man's voice coming from downstairs, not her father, since he responded. Oh Lord, who was here now? Did she have to face someone from the family? Uncle Spiro?

Her father's voice was hushed, unusually so. Her mother said something, too, but then the man spoke again, and Agnes was drawn to the door and into the tiny hall, needing to hear it.

Instantly, she recognized the broken English, the accent of a very recent arrival. Someone who'd been in America for only a month. Someone who thought she was...*omorfi*.

What is Nikodemus Santorini doing here?

She took a few more steps, clutching the strap of the bag on her shoulder, listening to the exchange, getting only bits and pieces of the conversation, mostly because the blood in her head was thumping like a drum.

"It is my decision, sir." De-*see*-sian. The Greek inflection sounded like music on his lips. What was his decision?

"No, I'm sorry, young man," her father said. "Your uncle would not forgive me."

Would not forgive him for what? What did Nik Santorini want? Why had he come here after she told him exactly who and *what* she was?

She put her hand on the banister rail and tiptoed down the attic steps, her legs quaking like they were made of Mama's jelly candy.

"May I see her?"

"No," her father said.

"Yes." Her mother's sharp response was just as fast and accompanied by her footfalls at the bottom of the next flight of stairs. "I'll get her."

"I'm right here, Mama," she whispered as they met almost in the middle.

"He's…here," her mother said, breathless. "I think he said he saw you? He met you? He…"

"He knows everything," Agnes said, almost strangled by the hope that gripped her throat. "So why is he here?"

"He wants to—"

"Give flowers to my betrothed." He stood at the bottom of the steps, holding a massive bunch of roses and greens. "A boo…boo…"

"Bouquet," she whispered.

"Bouquet." He smiled, and suddenly it felt like the dimly lit stairway was bathed in sunlight.

"To welcome her home."

She floated down the last few stairs, not sure if her feet actually touched the wood. Her gaze was locked on his, her heart pounding so loud it should have echoed in the hall. She let the suitcase slide down her arm and thud to the step.

"Nik…" She stopped on the last step, eye to eye with him. "Did you understand what I told you? Was I clear? Should my father say it in Greek? I am—"

He put a hand out and touched his fingers to her lips, silencing her. "You are my betrothed, Agnes. I will have you. I will love you."

"But…will you forgive me?" How was that even possible?

His smile was slow, dear, and so very genuine. "I already have."

She managed a slow, unsteady breath, taking the flowers and letting their fingers touch for the first time. The first of many times, she hoped.

Her father appeared in the doorway, his scowl firmly in place. "Agnes is not welcome in this house," he said.

"Baba!"

"Estevan!"

Even Nik gave him a look of utter dismay.

"Out." He pointed to the door. "You have brought disgrace on this home."

All the joy that had bubbled up seeped out of her like a slow leak in a balloon. How could he? Nik had forgiven her. Couldn't her father do the same?

"You cannot do that." Nik ground out the words, an undercurrent of anger in every syllable.

"I can and I will. I am the father."

"And I will be the husband," he said without taking his gaze off Baba.

"You will leave and never come back," Baba said. "To take her is to excuse her."

Nik shook his head, then turned back to Agnes. "You will live with my aunt and uncle until we are married," Nik said, gesturing toward the door. "I'll take you there."

Behind her, she could hear her mother sobbing. Next to her, she could see her father fuming. And in front of her stood the man she knew that she would someday love, if she didn't already.

He reached for her suitcase with one hand and her arm with the other.

Without a word, they walked out into the sunshine to begin a life together.

Chapter Eleven

"I can't stop thinking about your story, Agnes." Finnie leaned over after handing a little boy a sizable box, knowing the toy inside would meet his request to Santa for a tractor that made noise. "It takes a very big man to forgive like that."

"He was big, and great, and as he got older, he had a temper that occasionally flared and a booming voice that scared children, but deep inside, he was kind."

"A saint," Finnie agreed. "Did you ever know why he did that for you?"

"He claimed he loved me at first sight, but I think he was just one of those men who has a tender heart for the broken. I was very, very lucky."

"I can't believe you never told anyone, not even your son."

"Why would I?" Agnes adjusted the itchy beard that stuck to the remnants of her lipstick, ready to be done with the story and get back to Christmas. "Now how did you know that the last gift had a tractor in it. Are you sure of that?"

Finnie picked up another box from the pile and pointed to tiny letters hidden in the wrapping that said *baby doll.* "'Tis a secret," she said, shaking the strip of sleigh bells she held to greet each child. The ringing matched her laughter. "And why I spent much of November wrapping presents at church."

"Now it makes sense," Agnes muttered. "I thought you'd taken a lover in your Bible study."

"Speaking of taking lovers, did your father ever come around?"

Agnes sighed. "He didn't, no. He refused to attend our wedding, and about a year later, Nik and I moved to Chestnut Creek, because seeing him in Astoria just tore me apart. Not long after we moved, my father had a heart attack and died."

"He died because his heart didn't work properly," Finnie said with a wry look. "I'm sorry."

"I'm happy to say that my mother and my sisters, once free of his heavy hand, reconciled with me and came to Nico's christening. My in-laws moved from Greece, too, and lived in Chestnut Creek. They were wonderful grandparents to my son."

"Did you ever see Norman Anderson again?" Finnie asked, a little tentative as if the answer worried her.

Agnes nodded, remembering the day she saw him shopping at the perfume counter at Macy's about fifteen years ago. "I did," she said. "I had gone up to Astoria to visit my sister Irene, and we took a shopping trip to the city. I didn't even recognize him when he said my name."

"No!" Finnie's mouth dropped. "What happened to him?"

She gave into a wry smile. "Fifty pounds, no hair, and he was shopping for a gift for his third wife."

She snorted. "That's what happened to Norman Anderson."

"Then you were lucky in so many ways," Finnie said, jingling her bells with happiness at this news. "So it all worked out in the end."

Until...the real end. Agnes put the thought away as the next child came forward. Pyggie and Gala, looking fine in their elf sweaters and knit caps, got up to greet the little boy with their barks and get the treat that Agnes offered.

"Merry Christmas, laddie." Gramma reached out her white gloved hands, welcoming as always, tender in touch and voice. It was a gift, really. "Come and sit on my dear husband's lap. Tell him what you'd be wantin' him to bring you this year."

The boy narrowed his eyes at Agnes. "I think that's a lady Santa."

"'Tis the only Santa out here in Bushrod Square givin' away gifts," Gramma quipped. "But you don't have to sit on Santa's lap, child. Just tell us what you're hoping for this Christmas."

"I want to be on the Little League team," he said, kicking the ground. "But the coach doesn't like me."

"Well, we can't make him like you," Agnes said with a shrug.

With a quick look to quiet Agnes, Finnie leaned in and said, "But we can help you get so good at yer game that he's beggin' you to be on the team."

"You can?" Brown eyes widened.

"Hand me the long one, Santa," she said to Agnes. "Right there with the red-and-white striped paper."

Agnes reached into the pile and nearly dislodged one of her fat pillows, clutching her fake stomach with one hand and pulling a long skinny box from the bottom. On the side was written *bat with ball*.

"That's the one," Finnie said, taking it and handing it to the child. "I think this might help your game, lad."

His eyes widened. "Is it a bat?"

"Don't spoil your surprise," Agnes said.

But Finnie waved her hand to quiet Agnes's reprimand. "The surprise is going to be on your coach's face when you hit home runs!"

"I'm not that good."

"But ye will be. That there is a magic stick, lad. The more you swing it, the more it hits. Try it."

He took the package gingerly, a smile threatening. "Magic?"

"Christmas magic," Finnie assured him.

"Thank you." He clutched the box to his chest and turned to run to his mother and announce he'd been given magic.

"How do you do it?" Agnes marveled. "How is it that being kind comes so naturally to you?"

Finnie laughed. "'Tis a bit difficult to be churlish with a child at Christmas, Agnes, even for you."

She put her hand on Finnie's arm. "Why can't I change? I'm trying so hard."

Finnie put a hand on Agnes's velvet-clad arm. "Sweet lass, you carry too much shame. The Lord forgives you, your husband forgave you, and your life went on, better than before, despite what Norman Anderson did to you. Let go of your shame, and you'll find it much easier to smile. Here, try it on this next boy."

She did, on him and several others, until there was a short break in the line of kids, but nothing about being kind felt natural. And yet, she had to change, and quickly. And she also had to find...Charis.

"Ah, look who's here." Finnie pointed over the head of the next departing child as Pru walked toward them, pushing a baby carriage with the top pulled securely down. "'Tis the baby Jesus himself. How did it go, lass?"

"Well, he did wail a little bit when one of the wisemen screamed his line right in Danny's face, but for the most part, he was divine." She laughed at the pun. "So to speak. How's the Claus family doing?"

"Have a wee break in the action," Finnie said. "I think we'll be able to leave when your mother arrives. Then we—"

"My doggies!" A little girl called out from a few passersby, tugging on the hand that held her, reaching out to Pyggie and Gala. "Those are my doggies! My friends!"

Agnes immediately recognized her as the child who'd been so in love with the dogs at the coffee tent earlier in the day. Pru's friend's little sister. A fact that was confirmed by the look on Pru's face as the girl broke free and ran toward them.

"Pyggie and Gala!" She folded onto the snow-covered grass, practically tackling the dogs.

"Avery!" Pru's friend Teagan came forward. "We're not stopping here."

"Hey, Teag," Pru said quickly. "It's okay. She can play with the dogs."

"I want to sit on Santa's lap! I want to ask for my special gift."

"Not now, Avery." Teagan reached down to get the girl, but Pru put a hand on her friend's arm.

"It's fine, Teagan. Just because you're mad at me doesn't mean she can't sit on Santa's lap."

Teagan tipped her head in resignation. "Two minutes, Avery. I'll be right over there."

Pru's face paled with disappointment that Agnes felt in her own chest. The girl didn't miss a beat, though.

"Right this way, Avery," she said softly. Gently nudging the little girl closer to Santa with one hand and rolling her little brother's stroller with the other, Pru exhibited the same grace that her mother and great-grandmother seemed to exude. "You can sit on Santa's lap, if you like."

"I want to!" she cried out, flipping back strawberry-blond curls as she fearlessly approached Agnes. "I want to tell Santa what he has to bring me."

Entitled little brat. But Agnes forced a smile and reached out her hands, settling the little girl on her knee and leaning her into the big pillows that made her stomach.

"Ho ho ho, little one." She attempted her deep Santa voice, shooting Pru a look when she giggled a few feet away.

Finnie merrily jingled her strip of sleigh bells. "Merry Christmas, Avery. Would you like to tell Santa what you want to celebrate Jesus's birthday?"

She crossed her arms and looked around, and all three of them followed the child's gaze. It landed on Teagan, who was a good forty feet away, looking at her phone.

"You can't give me what I want," she said, all her bravado suddenly gone.

Finnie and Agnes exchanged a look of surprise.

"Well, give us a chance to try," Agnes said. "You'd be surprised what Mrs. Claus can dig out of her pile of goodies."

The little girl shook her head, and tears threatened.

"Avery." Pru came closer and crouched next to Agnes's lap. "What's the matter, honey?"

The lower lip came out. "My daddy moved away for good."

Pru sucked in a breath. "Are you sure? Maybe he took a trip." She looked up at Agnes and mouthed, "I never heard that," over Avery's head.

"He took all his suitcases and money."

"He took his money?" Agnes asked, shocked by the phrase.

"He told Mommy he hates her, and he isn't coming back, and now we can't have Christmas!" Teardrops fell now, making Pru stand up and block the child from anyone's view—including her sister, who was still staring at her phone.

"I don't know about that, Avery," Pru said gently. "Maybe the grownups are talking about things you don't understand."

She shook her head vehemently. "He's gone, and we're not getting our Christmas present."

"What was the present?" Finnie asked, riveted like Agnes and Pru to the child's story.

"A dog. Like that one." She pointed to Gala. "A wiener dog! He said we could have one, but then he left, and Mommy said there isn't going to be a dog." Tears rolled down her freckled cheeks. "I want a wiener dog," she choked on a sigh. "It's all I want in the whole wide world, Santa." She pressed herself against Agnes. "Please give me one of yours."

Agnes blinked, speechless. "Well, I...I... Those are my..."

Finnie quickly turned to the pile. "Lass, I have one here that's just as good. Not a wiener dog, not alive, but this plush boy will snuggle next to you all night long."

The little girl looked at the box Finnie offered and took it with a reluctant sigh. "Okay. My sister said we're not getting any presents 'cause Mommy doesn't have any money."

"Oh." Pru put her hand over her mouth. "I had no idea." She looked past Avery to where her friend had been standing, but now Teagan marched toward them, her expression unreadable.

"Come on, Avery," Teagan said, sliding past the baby carriage to get close to Agnes. "Thank the ladies for your present. Mom just texted, and we have to go."

"Is Daddy home?" she asked with painfully bright enthusiasm.

"No, he's not ever..." She caught herself and glanced at Pru, whose face was pure sympathy. "Look, I'm sorry," she added on a whisper to Pru. "I couldn't get you anything, and I was embarrassed, and...it doesn't matter. My mom says we're moving to Raleigh next week to live with my grandmother. So, see ya, Pru."

"Teagan!" Pru stood and started to reach for her friend, but the other girl shrugged off the hug.

"Avery. Let's go." She snagged the little girl's arm and tugged her away. As she stumbled off, clinging to her present, Avery turned and looked at Agnes. "Are you sure I can't have one of your dogs? Please, please, please? I want a wiener dog!"

Something welled up in Agnes. Pity. Sadness. Maybe Christmas spirit. She opened her mouth, but Finnie put a hand on her arm. "You don't have to be that nice," she whispered. Then, "Just be a good girl, Avery, and be nice to your sister. Santa will be back next year."

"But she won't." Pru folded to the ground in front of Agnes. "She's moving? Her parents are splitting up? She couldn't afford a gift for me? Why didn't she tell me all that?"

"It's her shame," Agnes said, throwing a look at Finnie.

"What do you mean, Yiayia?"

"I mean that sometimes a person cloaks themselves with cruelty so they don't have to face the pity and judgment of others. Believe me, I know."

"I guess." Pru sighed. "I wouldn't have pitied or judged her, and I don't care about a present. I just want my friend back."

"I understand," Agnes said. "I really do."

Pru started to push up to stand, but she paused midway and gave a long, hard look to Agnes. "Do you really think that's what it was?"

"Absolutely. It's what I do," she added. "As my good friend Finnie has pointed out."

"Why are you ashamed?" Pru asked. "You liked a boy enough to run after him, but you married the one your dad wanted for you, right? It all worked out, and you have nothing to be ashamed of. Or did I miss something?"

"You—"

"Didn't miss a thing," Finnie interjected. "She left that restaurant and took the subway back home, realizing her mistake, and married the handsome, wonderful man who was the father to Nico."

None of that was a lie, Agnes realized. It's just that Finnie left out the part about spending a month in the bed of a married man. Gratitude and a deep, deep love for Finola Kilcannon rolled over her.

"Oh." Pru leaned back on her heels. "Then why do you think shame has made you cruel, which you are not, by the way?"

"Have you asked your grandfather's new wife about that?" she asked, referring to the woman who was once her daughter-in-law. "Katie will tell you just how cruel I can be, and her only fault was not being Greek."

"Well, you're not cruel anymore, Yiayia, so you need to quit worrying about it."

Agnes sighed heavily. "I do worry about it. And I needed the dog we spent the day trying to get as much as that little girl. More."

"Why?" Pru frowned and looked at Finnie, who just shrugged.

"Don't ask me, lass. Agnes is cryptic about some things."

"I'm not cryptic. I'm..." Agnes sat back and looked from one to the other, making her decision, knowing that one last secret could help these two and explain a lot to them. "When we're done here, before your mother gets here, I'll tell you. I hope you'll understand and not think I'm crazy."

"I don't think you're crazy or cruel or anything but wonderful." Pru hugged her hard. "And you helped me figure out what happened with my friend."

She planted an unexpected kiss on Agnes's cheek, making her laugh. "Thank you, Yiayia."

"You're welcome, Prudence." She leaned back and patted the young girl's cheek. "I hope you feel that way after I finish my story."

Chapter Twelve

Jacaranda Lakes, Florida 2018

"What's the matter, Agnes?" Linda Jurgenson leaned her skinny seventy-seven-year-old frame against Agnes's arm. "You don't look so good today."

"I'm damn near eighty, Linda." Actually a little past, but none of her Golden Girl pals needed to know that. "How good can I look?"

The truth was, Agnes felt like hell today and had very little interest in the weekly luncheon her canasta team seemed to love. She hadn't slept due to indigestion, had a headache that could kill a cow, and now she was forced to eat a lunch cooked by pimply-faced teenage boys using a can of tomato sauce shipped from a corporate office. Not how a *good* restaurant ran. Not how she and Nik had run Santorini's.

"You are a little pale," Barbara "I'll Stop Any Fight Before It Happens" Riley chimed in. "Did you skip your rouge?"

"No one calls it 'rouge' anymore, Barbara. You're giving away your old age," Agnes shot back. "And no, I didn't skip it."

Carol Burns looked up from her usual examination of every single breadstick in the basket, as if there was some kind of prize for getting the best one. "You just miss Ted," she said. "It's been, what? Two months without a word? That's gotta hurt. Oh, what the hell." She plucked one stick in each hand. "I guess I'll take two. That's why they invented 'unlimited' on the menu."

"If I'm pale, it's because I hate chain restaurants."

"But this is Olive Garden." Linda looked scandalized. "We all can agree on Italian."

Agnes rolled her eyes. "We all can agree that the food is trash, and the service sucks."

"Agnes!" Barbara chided her. "It's not about the food. This is canasta team-bonding time."

"You want to bond? Eat the alfredo sauce. It's made of Elmer's glue, or at least that's what it tastes like. That'll bond you up but good."

Barbara chuckled, but she laughed at everything everyone said. No discernment, that one.

"Well, I for one am having creamy mushroom ravioli," Carol said, closing her menu with a flourish. "It's almost as good as sex."

Barbara snorted, Linda pretend-gasped, but Agnes felt just lousy enough to call the little liar on it.

"Really, Carol? You remember sex? From, what? When Richard Nixon was president?"

The other woman narrowed her blue eyes. "You really are missing Ted, aren't you?"

"No, I was bitchy before he picked me over you, believe me."

She nearly choked on her bite of bread. "Agnes, you flatter yourself if you think I was jealous."

"Please." More irritation rolled around Agnes's gut, burning a little more than her usual constant bickering with Carol caused. "You were the shade of that fake tree when he asked me to the Sabal Palms Valentine Dance."

Carol sniffed and slathered some butter on her next bite of bread. "I'll admit I thought he was nice enough, considering how slim the pickings are at that complex, and the man played a decent shuffleboard game, which I suppose made him good at…other things."

"Hubba, hubba," Barbara chimed in, earning a dark look from Agnes.

But Linda leaned in to whisper, "I did notice that day we played charades in the clubhouse that he had very large hands. You know what they say about a man with large hands."

"He can carry two bags of trash at once," Barbara joked.

"The only thing he could carry was a lottery ticket," Agnes said, shaking her head.

"No kidding," Carol said. "A million dollars in a scratch-off. Talk about lucky."

They all moaned a little, Agnes more so than anyone. Not that she wanted old Ted "forever," but it stung that the minute he got all that cash, he headed off to buy his grandson a farm in Iowa, then stayed there with him.

The waitress came over to get their order, and Agnes asked to go last, staring at the menu, but the letters and pictures just swam in front of her eyes. What she wouldn't do for a good plate of moussaka instead of this junk. And a...

A weird pain in her shoulder pinched, a little more intense than it had been this morning, making her wince.

"Are you okay, Agnes?" Barbara asked.

"Just dreading this food."

The waitress inched back in surprise. "Have you had a bad experience here, ma'am?"

"'Have I ever *not* had a bad experience?' is a better question." The shoulder pain zinged down her arm as she closed the menu. "I guess I'll have the mushroom ravioli, but tell the chef, which is being generous about whatever prepubescent is back there, that less is more on that sauce."

The young woman gave a tight smile, but her eyebrows raised as if she'd had it with cranky customers.

So sue me if I want my lunch to taste like actual food.

"Do you have to be so snappy with the poor girl?" Carol asked when she left. "She doesn't make the ravioli."

"Carol." Agnes inched closer and flinched again as the pain found a new home under her collarbone. "I ran a restaurant for most of my adult life. The service person is the face, voice, and presentation of the place to the customers. It won't kill her to deliver the message to the line cook."

"It won't kill her," Linda said softly. "But it might kill you."

"What the heck is that supposed to mean?" Agnes shot back.

"What she's trying to say is being unkind just shortens your life-span, Agnes." Barbara reached over and patted Agnes's hand. "It causes stress that breaks down the strands of your DNA."

"Someone's been bingeing *Dr. Oz*," Agnes muttered.

"She's trying to help you," Carol said.

Agnes reached to pick up her iced tea, but a brand-new wave of pain shot down her arm, and this one was accompanied by a band around her chest. "Don't gang up on..." Her breath grew so tight, she couldn't talk for a moment. "Me," she finished, suddenly aware her upper lip was wet.

"Honey, you really don't look good," Linda said with real alarm in her voice. "You're sweating."

"Because it's hotter than the basement of hell in here." She squeezed her eyes shut as another pain sliced through her shoulder.

"What's wrong?"

"I think she's going to faint."

"Agnes, open your eyes."

Shut up! Shut up! Shut... She willed her lips to move and say the words, but they wouldn't. Nothing would move. Not her arm or her mouth or anything. All her muscles seized up and gripped her as a wave of nausea roiled through her body.

She tried to breathe and tamp it down, but everything was so dark. And hot. And painful.

"Agnes!"

"Someone call 911!"

Why wouldn't they all shut up? Go away! Leave her alone! Let her...

She felt her face hit the table, and her last thought was, thank God she didn't go face first into that garbage ravioli.

Everything was so quiet. Not just silent, but more like Agnes had just stepped into a vacuum that sucked away all the noise. And light. And air. There was just...nothing.

So this is it? This is what all the fuss is about? A big fat black hole of blackness?

She knew all the clouds and angels were a bunch of crap. She knew it! No harps. No pearly gates. No stinking light at the end of the tunnel. No reason to wallow in guilt and shame because it was all...over.

Or was it?

Agnes pushed up and started to move forward in the darkness—not walking exactly, but, well, yeah, floating, with no idea where she was going or why. At least the pain stopped. All of it, actually. Her old back didn't ache, her dry eyes didn't burn, and her right knee felt like someone had magically removed all of the arthritis that had made it scream with every step.

That was nice.

But everything else was...nothing. Was this what the other place was, then? Just nothing? Guess that beat—

A noise cracked and echoed. A sharp, sudden, loud...bark? No, that couldn't have been what she heard.

She took a few more steps, her arms out like a blind person, vaguely aware that whatever was around her—it wasn't air—was like a blanket made of satin and…peace. Yes, this all felt rather—

There it was again. Definitely a bark or someone calling out with a very low voice. She turned, but it was just as black back there and all around her. There was nothing. Just—

Something brushed her leg, and she opened her mouth to scream, but no noise came out. No air, either. She wasn't breathing. But it didn't matter.

She bent over slowly and reached down, her hands suddenly hitting something small and wiggly and…furry.

Was this Gala? Much too thin to be Pyggie. She wanted to say the dog's name, but she couldn't make a sound. She couldn't see. She couldn't…good heavens, her feet were not touching anything.

Was she flying?

The dog barked again, and instinct made Agnes close her fist around a collar and let him lead her…somewhere. For a long time, it was just more blackness. They walked, maybe glided, maybe floated, she didn't know and, honestly, didn't care. The air was sweet and gentle, and the whole place was dark, but…like sheer contentment wrapped around her.

Then she saw the light. A pinpoint at first, like a tiny laser beam a hundred miles away. The dog saw it, too, barking again and urging her forward. It felt like she was running now, still not actually touching anything under her feet, no air brushing by, and no need to even catch her breath.

She had no breath. But somewhere, far away, like a million miles, she heard something hiss. A soft, distant scream. A man's voice delivering a rough order. The sound of chaos and…death.

Wherever she was now, the body she left behind just expired.

For the first time, Agnes got scared, but the light point had grown exponentially, shedding a yellow-gold beam and finally letting her see that she was in a long, long hallway, and her companion was a small brown short-haired dachshund. Not Pyggie or Gala, but…

"Charis."

She heard the word, distinct and close, and looked from side to side to hear who'd spoken it. The voice wasn't male or female or familiar or…human.

"Charis."

The dog barked, suddenly slowing down to paw at Agnes. Charis. *Is that your name, puppy?* She thought the question and got a bark and wagging tail in response.

Charis.

Still drawn to the golden light, she tried to remember what the word *charis* meant in Greek, letting her mind slip back to classes she took on Sundays after church. *Charis*…meant grace, mercy, forgiveness. The root of charity. The act of kindness. A gift freely given, like grace, mercy, and forgiveness.

Was she getting all that after all?

Joy, tangible and unfamiliar, shot through her with an otherworldly kind of power. She was! She was getting *charis*!

The dog barked and howled as if he could read her thoughts and wanted to confirm this fact. This little dachshund was her escort to heaven! Agnes knew that to be so without a shadow of a doubt, soaring toward the light that was growing brighter, bolder, whiter, and closer.

She followed the furry body, her eyes on his snout and floppy ears. Charis was taking her to heaven.

Nico would be there! The thought of her son, yanked from life by cancer before he could even see one of his children married, made her fly faster. And Nik. Nikodemus Santorini with his big voice and even bigger heart. Of course he'd be here. And Mama and...Baba. Maybe Baba. She hoped so. She hoped they were all there, waiting for her on the other side of that light.

The dog barked. *Yes, Charis, yes. Take me there!*

And suddenly, they stopped. So close to the light Agnes could reach out and touch it, but her arm wouldn't move. Neither would her legs. Everything stopped.

Please, can I go in?

The dog took a few steps forward, bathed in golden light, looking up with sweet brown eyes that said it all. All the nasty words, all the short tempers, all the cold manipulations, all the times she'd made herself safe and distant and...rotten.

She could see it all in that dog's eyes. And he was saying...*do better.*

But it's too late! I can't do better. I can't...I'm dead now!

A searing pain shot through her shoulder, like a white-hot poker stabbed directly through her lungs. Something pressed on her face, cold and wet, forcing air into her chest. A man's voice spoke unintelligible words, loud and furious, at her. She could taste metal and smell death, and everything hurt *so much she could not bear it.*

She was going to hell. It was so clear now. She was going to the wrong place, where there was no Nico or Nik or Mama. Paying for every unkind word. Every short response. Every ugly, nasty thing she'd ever done after a lifetime of doing so many. The only person there would be...*Norman Anderson.* No! *No, don't make me pay forever.* Not him, not that!

She got one last glimpse of the dog who had such promise and hope in his sweet little face.

Please take me, Charis. Take me to that light and—

Her body shook as if someone had stomped on her chest.

"Is she alive? Did that work?" Carol's voice floated around her head.

"Back off, ma'am, we're trying again. She's been clinically dead for six minutes, but..."

"Ready?"

"Ready. Clear!"

Whoompf! A force jolted her so hard she felt like her arms had been yanked from her body. Electricity zipped through her veins, sparking and hot. And she sucked in a breath so deep and sharp, it should have burst her lungs.

And suddenly, she could see. A man inches from her face and another one right next to him. And the ceiling of Olive Garden.

Oh no. She was on the floor at Olive Garden?

No, on a stretcher. And there were so many people gathered around. Voices. Noises. Sirens.

"She's awake! We have a pulse!"

A roar that sounded like she was standing in Madison Square Garden deafened her. Someone squealed. Someone sobbed. Someone muttered thanks to God.

Finally, her eyes focused on the man in front of her. Young, with blue eyes and dark hair.

"Welcome back, Agnes," he said, his voice gentle and warm. "You're quite a lucky lady. You get another chance at all this."

Another chance. *Another chance?*

This time, she'd do better. This time, she'd be kind and loving and sweet. This time, she'd treat other people…differently.

And then next time…would Charis take her to the light?

She blinked, unable to talk due to the oxygen mask pressing on her face. But now she had complete clarity.

"Now let's get you to the hospital, ma'am. You've survived a heart attack that would have killed most people. Must not be your time yet."

But…when would her time come? And would she be ready? Would she get into the light?

She didn't know. But she did know that whatever time she had, Agnes Mastros Santorini would be a changed woman, inside and outside. And while she was on this earth, she would find Charis, who would be a constant reminder to…do better.

But what did that mean? It had to be more than a kind word. It had to be more than holding her tongue. Wasn't the very idea of grace and charity to not hold a person accountable, to have mercy? Then why had she come back?

Because she had a purpose on this earth.

But what was it?

As they rolled her into the back of an ambulance, Carol and Linda and Barbara walked along, all of them cooing and crying. Agnes managed to lift her fingers in a halfhearted wave, which sent them all into another bout of sobbing.

They cared about her that much? That was more than just tears about the struggle to find a good canasta sub.

Yes, there were people who cared about her. A family in North Carolina, for starters. A daughter-in-law who ached for the loss of Nico as much as Agnes did and five beautiful grandchildren. And Pyggie and Gala.

And...Charis.

That dog was...her guide. She had to find him, and he would lead her to her purpose. And in the meantime, just in case, she had to do better.

Chapter Thirteen

"There's Mom." Pru pointed toward the opening of the coffee tent where the three of them sat, huddled with the stroller, sipping hot chocolate and listening to Yiayia's jaw-dropping story. "Is there more?" she asked as she threw a wave to her mother.

"More?" Gramma wiped her eyes under her glasses. "This old heart can't take any more."

Yiayia managed a smile. "Now you know why I showed up in Bitter Bark, and the whole Santorini clan claimed I'd changed, and it wasn't just the thirty-some pounds I lost to save my ticker."

"You have changed," Pru said. "I mean, I didn't know you before, but I can't even imagine you talking to your friends the way you describe."

"That's just part of it," Yiayia said.

"And the dog?" Pru asked. "I get that's why you wanted Rover, because it sounds like he was a dead ringer for this Charis, but what's he going to do? Take you back there?"

"Remind me of how I should act."

"If it's real, 'tis not an act," Gramma whispered.

"And do you really need a reminder?" Pru asked. "I mean, Gramma Finnie's pretty good at keeping you on track, and sometimes it seems Cassie is, too."

"Cassie knows. I told her the story when we were stuck in the basement that day she broke her foot and I thought I had another heart attack," Yiayia said. "But I've always felt that finding the dog was part of why I was sent back. Maybe that's my purpose. Maybe he'll lead me to it."

Finnie leaned closer. "Agnes, we discussed your purpose the day we decided to live together. You told me your purpose is to help me find fairy-tale endings for all of our many grandchildren, remember?" She added a sly grin. "We're two-for-two, and I really think we need to work on Connor."

"Connor?" Pru snorted. "Man, you Dogmothers like a challenge. Connor Mahoney is so single, it hurts. Plus, do you really think there's a woman in Bitter Bark whose heart he hasn't smashed?"

The conversation ended as Pru's mother came over, rubbing her hands together in anticipation. "Where's my little superstar?"

"He was awesome, Mom."

"I heard! I just ran into some people who were at the play. They said he'll be getting a Tony for sure." Her laugh faded as she got closer and eyed the three of them. "You guys don't exactly look mired in Christmas cheer. Everything okay?"

"Right as rain, lass." Gramma pushed up, adjusting her Mrs. Claus jacket. "But we're terribly late for Christmas Eve dinner."

"We can go straight there, unless you want to go home and change."

"Our party clothes are on under this." Yiayia rubbed the red velvet, sagging now that she'd taken out her pillow belly. "But I have to admit, it's been warm and comfy."

"Great." Mom reached into the carriage. "I know he's sleeping, but..." She picked up the baby and nuzzled him, her eyes sparking as they always did when she held him. "I missed my little guy. And..." She winked at Pru. "My little girl. Things any better, hon?"

"I saw Teagan," she said. "I'll tell you everything in the car on the way to Waterford. Are all our presents packed?"

"Some are in my car, and your dad took the rest over." She gently eased the baby, who was still sleeping, back into the stroller. "Come on, girls. It's Christmas Eve!"

The three of them exchanged a sort of sad smile, and Pru fought a sigh. Yiayia's story was amazing, but a little scary. What if she didn't get to go back? What if she should have had the dog? What if...what if Pru never saw Teagan again?

This just didn't feel like a spectacular Christmas, but she did her best to hide that from her mom.

It wasn't that difficult once they got to Waterford Farm. Like every other Christmas in Pru's entire life, the homestead on a hundred acres that also included one of the best canine rescue and training facilities in the state was decked out for the holiday and rocking with a houseful of family.

But this year it looked *extraordinary*.

As they walked into the kitchen, already packed and noisy, Pru's mother sucked in a soft breath and stopped, taking it all in. There were uncles, aunts, and cousins everywhere, lights flickering in every room, and plenty of the beloved Jameson's flowing for the adults. Christmas carols rang from speakers no one could see, platters of food were spread on every surface, and the sound of raucous, happy laughter and barking dogs echoed through every room of the rambling farmhouse.

"What is it, Mom?" Pru whispered.

"It's so…different this year."

It was, but she couldn't quite figure out why. "Well, there are more of us, that's for sure, since Grandpa married Katie Santorini."

"It's not just that." Mom looked at her with sparkly tears in her eyes. "We've had some good Christmases the last few years."

"Well, last year we were in a cabin in the mountains giving birth to puppies," Pru reminded her sheepishly, since that was all Pru and Gramma Finnie's fault.

"And the year before, we pretended to lose a puppy because Aidan came home from Afghanistan."

Pru nodded, smiling. "That was a good Christmas, too."

"But this…"

Grandpa Daniel came over to greet them, a smile stretched across his face. He always looked like that now, ever since he met Katie and finally healed from the loss of Grannie Annie.

"That's the difference," Molly whispered. "He's happy again."

"Merry Christmas to my beautiful girls." He enveloped them both in a huge hug. "What do you think about this place, huh? Did Katie do amazing things, Molls?"

"She did, Dad." Mom inched back and put her hand on Grandpa's cheek, her eyes all full of affection like when she picked up baby Danny or looked at Pru's father. "She did amazing things for you."

Grandpa's smile faltered. "Don't make me tear up on Christmas Eve," he warned, turning to the stroller. "Now, where's my little namesake?"

While they fussed over the baby, Pru slipped away to give a hug to cousin Ella, who was technically her second cousin, possibly once removed—they could never figure it out. Whatever, she was looking festive in a gold top with her short hair spiked and giant ornament earrings dangling to her shoulders.

"You're rockin' it, Smella," she teased, using the nickname only Ella's three older brothers could usually get away with.

Ella gave Pru a sideways look. "And I see you made no effort," she teased.

"I was in charge of baby Jesus at the church play," she said on a laugh. "And I've been traipsing around Bitter Bark all day on a wild goose—er, dog chase."

"A dog?" Cassie, along with her brand-new husband, Braden, came up to join them. "Why were you chasing a dog?"

"You know, that dachshund Yiayia wants, but we didn't get him."

Cassie turned to say something to Braden, but Pru put her hand on her arm. "Cass, your mom has made a big difference here. Tonight feels really special."

"I was just saying that," Braden said. "I haven't

seen this many lights in Waterford on Christmas Eve since…" He gave a sad smile.

"Since my aunt Annie died," Ella finished, putting her arm around Cassie. "The Santorinis are a good addition to this Irish mess, don't you think, Pru?"

"I do," she agreed, turning when little Christian powered into the room and came right at her.

"Pwu! Wait till you see—"

"Shhh!" Cassie grabbed his shoulder. "It's a surprise for *everyone*."

"A surprise?" Pru choked softly. "Last time you had a surprise, it was your wedding."

She looked up at Braden, one of Pru's absolute favorite cousins. A firefighter like his brothers, Connor and Declan, Braden had a heart of gold and an easy laugh. "It's nothing that shocking, right, Einstein?" Cassie teased.

"It's pretty shocking," he said on a laugh, giving Christian's head a rub. "And mum's the word, or Santa will be really upset."

Christian's eyes narrowed. "Santa's not—"

Ella bent over and got right in his face. "Oh yes, he is, baby cakes, so don't even think about saying what you're about to say. You have little bitty cousins now, and only believers get what they ask for."

He smirked a little as his dad, Uncle Liam, and his mom, Aunt Andi, came over with wee Fee, as they called baby Fiona, toddling between them in a green velvet dress. They started talking about the elf parade, then Shane and Chloe came over with Connor.

"We need an elf parade in Bitter Bark," Andi said. "It sure would be easier than driving to Holly Hills every year."

127

"Yeah," Liam agreed. "Chloe, you should talk to your aunt. If Mayor Wilkins gets behind the idea, it'll happen."

Chloe let out a sigh. "Except next year, she won't be mayor."

"What?" At least three of them asked the question in unison.

"I thought she loved being the mayor," Andi said. "She took over when your uncle Frank died, and those were big mayor shoes to fill."

Chloe shrugged. "She's stepping down early next year."

"Who's going to replace her?" Liam asked.

"Field's wide open," Chloe replied. "I was thinking about asking Daniel."

"I'd run," Connor said. "I'd love to be mayor of this town."

Liam tilted his head, and Shane snorted. And the rest of them kind of stared in disbelief.

"You do know adult women, many of whom are your sworn enemies, can vote," Shane said.

Connor slid him a look. "Of course. Women love me."

"A little too much," Liam added with a wry smile.

Pru looked around the room as they joked, her gaze landing on Gramma Finnie and Yiayia, sitting side by side at the kitchen table, deep in conversation...and looking at Connor.

"Well, you better do something," Pru said, "because two crazy Dogmothers have got you in their sights."

The whole group laughed and hooted, but Cassie and Braden just grinned.

"Do not underestimate those women." Cassie pointed to her brother Alex, who stood in a corner whispering to Grace Donovan, his partner in everything...thanks to the Dogmothers.

"Nah, they're working on John," Connor said. "They know better than to try and tie me down."

"I think Declan should be next," Braden said. "He's the oldest Mahoney."

"I think *I* should be next," Ella said. "I'm the prettiest Mahoney and haven't had a date in ages."

"You're not allowed to date, Smella." Connor grinned at his sister. "'Cause none of us want to have to kill a guy."

She rolled her eyes and looked at Pru. "Count your blessings that you have no older brothers, Pru."

Katie and Daniel joined them, starting to usher everyone into the newly renovated living room for the official placement of the candle in the window, an old Irish Christmas Eve tradition, and gifts.

As they broke up, Cassie put a hand on Pru's arm. "Do me a favor and keep Gramma and Yiayia in here until everyone's settled. I want them to come in last."

"Why?"

"You'll see."

Knowing the family loved their Christmas surprises, Pru agreed and walked over to distract the grannies, while the rest of the family spilled into the center hall and the formal living room. The echoes of laughter rang through the house, along with a few barks from God knew how many dogs, all of whom had probably already claimed their spots on the living room floor.

"What are you two cooking up now?" Pru teased as

she sat down in a way that purposely blocked them from getting up.

"We're just wondering." Gramma Finnie rested her chin in her palm. "Ye think there's a woman over twenty-five and under forty who *hasn't* fallen hard for Connor?"

Pru gave a snort. "You better try some fresh blood, Gramma. He wants to run for mayor of Bitter Bark. He won't have time for romance."

The two women looked at each other. "Mayor of Bitter Bark!" they said in an excited whisper.

"Who could be the first lady?" Yiayia asked.

"Oh good gracious," Gramma said, suddenly noticing the room had emptied out. "I must light the candle. 'Tis the first time we'll be tellin' the tale of our family settlin' here to the Santorinis."

Yiayia gave her arm a gentle jab. "Finnie, you've told us all a hundred times. The long version."

Gramma turned to her friend and patted her face, undaunted. "Because I like ye, lass. Let's go."

"No, wait," Pru said, glancing over her shoulder for some kind of signal from Cassie. "Let them all get settled, and we'll slide in last. Everyone is so polite, you know they'll save us the comfy sofa."

"Don't be ridiculous," Gramma said, shooing her out of the way. "Let's go."

"Absolutely," Yiayia said. "I want to open presents."

There was no stopping these two when they wanted something, so Pru hoped it didn't cost her with Cassie, but she gave up and let them out. She followed them to the door of the family room, but before they got around the bottom of the stairs, Braden and Cassie came out from the center hall.

"There you are," he said, slyly getting behind Yiayia to put his hands over her eyes.

"What's this?" she demanded.

"Just let me lead you, Yiayia," he said, throwing a grin at Gramma and Pru. "Cassie told me what you wanted most for Christmas and…"

As Pru followed, she automatically reached for Gramma Finnie's hand as the first wisp of hope twirled through her.

Cassie knew.

"So we found the perfect present for you today."

Today. In the park. A young couple…

Just then, a little brown dachshund, wearing one of Gramma Finnie's red doggy scarves, came trotting out of the living room, and the whole family—and the dogs—miraculously stayed quiet, all of them watching.

Braden kept his hands over Yiayia's eyes, guiding her closer to the dog. She reached her hand out like a blind person…like maybe she did when she was in that dark place, walking toward the light.

Charis.

Pru glanced at Gramma, smiling through tears at the ones trailing down her great-grandmother's crinkled cheeks.

Cassie urged the dog closer, and as she did, he barked.

Yiayia gasped as if she recognized the sound, and Braden dropped his hands.

"Merry Christmas, Yiayia!" the whole clan hollered.

"His former owner called him Rover, if you can believe that," Cassie said.

"We had to give him a ticket to the Christmas play

that one of the other firemen gave me at work," Braden added.

But Yiayia just stood stone-still, staring at the dog. After a moment, she bent over, and he jumped into her arms, letting her lift him and press a kiss on his head.

Another cheer went up, and this time, the dogs gathered to bark along with everyone else, while a little bit of Christmas chaos ensued, which made it like every other Christmas Eve at Waterford Farm.

"Well, what do you know?" Gramma said as she inched closer to her friend. "You got your Christmas wish after all."

"I did." She closed her eyes and pressed her face into the dog's fur. "Charis."

"Charis?" Connor asked. "Is that what you're calling him?"

"Yes, it is."

"What does it mean?" a few people asked.

"There's one dog name I never heard," Grandpa said.

"Well, I, for one, love it." Alex grinned at his grandmother, then at the woman he'd recently fallen in love with. "It means 'grace' in Greek, so that's... perfection."

The women cooed, but Alex caught a little grief from his brother John and a few of the Mahoney men—but not, Pru noticed, the Kilcannons, who were all happily married.

The noise started up again as everyone moved into the living room, and Gramma lit the candle, told her story, and the presents and jokes started flying. The whole time, Yiayia held Charis on her lap.

"Good thing you left Pyggie and Gala at home to

rest," Pru whispered in her ear. "They'd be the color of Fee's dress with envy."

Yiayia just smiled, her gaze distant and content.

"But they'll get used to it," Pru added. "You'll spread the love."

She gave a long sigh. "Yes, I will. That's the lesson of this dog, you know. To spread the love."

Pru smiled. "I'm so glad you got your Christmas wish, Yiayia."

She didn't answer right away, listening to Liam handing out his usual Christmas gifts, T-shirts with dog sayings, including one for Shane, the world's greatest dog trainer, that said *Your dog doesn't know sit*, and another for Connor that read *Sorry, I can't. I have plans with my dog.*

"That ought to keep you out of trouble with the ladies," Liam joked.

"I don't even have a dog at the moment."

"Or a lady," Declan teased.

"You should talk, old man."

Yiayia gave out one more sigh, but it didn't sound as content as Pru would have thought, considering she was holding everything she'd said she wanted.

"How long does this go on?" she whispered to Pru.

"Until Midnight Mass, but we'll take a break to eat. Are you tired, Yiayia? Not everyone goes to Mass, so someone will take you home."

"I'm...not quite done today."

Pru gave her a look. "What do you mean?"

She leaned closer. "Can you get the keys to your mother's car?"

"My mother's...why? I can't drive you home."

"I want to leave."

133

"Leave the party? Now?"

"Wouldn't be the first time I slipped out on a holiday, now would it?" She added a playful wink.

"Where do you want to go?" Pru asked.

"To spread the love."

Pru just stared at her. "Where are you…"

She lifted one of Charis's floppy ears to cover her mouth and whisper, "How far away does your friend Teagan live?"

"Not ten minutes down the…" Pru blinked, then shook her head. "I'm not going over there now to beg for her…"

"No begging involved." Yiayia's gaze dropped to the dog, stroking his smooth brown head. "We have one more errand to run today, Pru. Santa has to deliver one last gift."

"Yiayia." She barely whispered the word. Chills exploded over her whole body as she realized what she meant. "You would do that?"

"I can't stop thinking about that little girl and how she loved playing with the dogs and…" She paused. "It's…*charis*. And my purpose. This Christmas, anyway."

"Oh." Pru put her hand over her mouth and blinked away tears. "What about Gramma Finnie?"

"Well, I'm not giving *her* away." At Pru's giggle, she added, "She'll come with us. Don't worry, I'll drive."

Pru smiled as a joy so deep she couldn't quite hold it in washed over her. "I love you, Yiayia. You are truly the Greek grandmother I never knew I needed but cannot live without."

"I love you, too, *koukla*."

"Hey…" Cassie leaned back from where she sat on the floor in front of them. "I hear you calling another girl 'koukla,' Yiayia."

"Because she's like another granddaughter to me. A great-granddaughter, in every sense of the word."

At the comment, the family grew quiet, and Katie reached over from where she perched on the arm of the chair where Grandpa Daniel sat. "You never cease to amaze me, Yiayia," she said softly. "You've changed so much."

Yiayia cleared her throat and leaned forward to the edge of the sofa, silencing everyone as they looked at her expectantly. "I hope that's true," she said. "In fact, I hope it so much that I'm now going to do the unthinkable and…" She lifted the dog in her arms a little higher. "Regift this little fellow."

"What?"

"Regift?"

"Yiayia, you don't want him?"

She smiled and waited until the barrage of questions slowed down. "I want him more than anything," she said. "But tonight, at the festival, I met a little girl whose life is taking an unhappy turn. She asked for a very specific gift…" Yiayia rubbed her hand over the dog's head. "And I feel she needs this sweet creature more than I do."

No one in the room said a word, Pru noticed. No one argued at the decision or cooed at the kindness or questioned her motives. Gramma Finnie simply put her hand on Yiayia's arm and smiled at her, silent in her complete approval.

Then Katie reached for her former mother-in-law again, her eyes misty. "Your son would be proud of that decision," she said, looking at Alex and John, and then at Cassie, who was wiping a tear. "It's fair to say all the Santorinis are very proud of you, Yiayia."

"Then, someone give me the keys to Santa's sleigh," she said quickly, dispelling the heavy emotion in the room. "Let's go, Finola, Prudence. We've got one more adventure tonight." She leaned close to Pru to whisper, "And who knows? Maybe you and your girlfriend can set things straight."

Chapter Fourteen

" I just texted Teagan," Pru said from the back seat, where she held Charis tight. "She hasn't answered, but she knows I'm coming over."

"Do you think it's too late, lass? 'Tis after ten on Christmas Eve."

"Never too late to get your Christmas wish, Finnie," Agnes chided, peering into the darkness as she drove Mom's SUV over the wet streets. They might have taken off as a trio with Charis, but Pru knew that at least one, two, or all of her uncles, aunts, and cousins were following at a distance to make sure they didn't got lost, have an accident, or otherwise repeat what happened last year.

But Yiayia *was* a better driver than Gramma Finnie, and this mission seemed to make her downright joyous. She hummed *Jingle Bells* and checked on Charis many times, assuring him that he was going to love his new home.

"Turn right here," Pru said, squinting into the woodsy side street where Teagan lived. "It's the third house, down a little ways."

"Oh, look, there is a light," Gramma Finnie said.

"That's Teagan's room," Pru told them, texting again as Yiayia pulled over. "I'm asking her to meet me at the door with her mom. If I get permission to give Avery the dog, you guys can do it." She tossed the Santa and Mrs. Claus jackets and the beard into the front. "Don't forget to dress the parts."

When Yiayia parked, Gramma turned and smiled at Pru, reaching back to give Charis a rub. "I'm gonna miss the wee thing," she said.

"Finnie. Don't second-guess." Yiayia shot her a look. "I know this is the right thing to do."

"Without a shadow of a doubt, Agnes," Gramma agreed, putting her arm on Yiayia's shoulder. "And I'm mighty proud of you, dear friend. 'Tis a sacrifice from your heart."

"Okay, here, take him." Pru slid the dog across the console and leaned over the driver's seat to give Yiayia a kiss. "You're the best Santa ever, you know that?"

"Ho ho...*go*." She gave a wink as she took Charis. "Now someone give me my beard."

Pru climbed out and started toward the house as the front light came on, and the door opened. She could see Teagan's narrow silhouette in an oversize sweatshirt and sleep pants.

"Pru, what are you doing here? What do you mean you have a dog?"

"Hey, Teag. My grandmothers want to give Avery the wiener dog she wants."

Behind her, Teagan's mom stepped into view, her curly blond hair mussed, but her eyes clear and bright. "Hello, Pru," she said. "Teagan told me."

"Is it okay, Mrs. Macdonald?" she asked. "Avery

really wants a dog, but we don't want to just thrust it on you if it isn't good for your family."

She smiled, those clear eyes misting up. "It's the nicest thing anyone's ever done, Pru. She fell asleep on the sofa watching the fireplace, certain Santa would be down the chimney with a dog. I tried to get her to bed, but she insisted on waiting." Her voice cracked. "I just don't know how to thank you for this."

"Aww, I'm glad." Pru smiled. "Then she'll never know that we skipped the chimney drop and had my great-grandmas come in the usual way." She turned and waved to the car, beckoning Yiayia and Gramma Finnie.

In a second, they climbed out, wearing their red velvet jackets, hats, and, oh yes, Yiayia wore her beard. And there was Charis, with his red scarf and floppy ears, hustling along on his little dachshund legs between them.

"Oh my God." Teagan put her hand over her mouth, tears springing to her eyes. "This is going to make her so happy."

Teagan and her mom put their arms around each other, then stepped out to greet and hug the grannies.

After a few more teary thank-yous and embraces, Gramma Finnie lifted the sleigh bells and started to ring them. "Let's go, Santa!" She gave Yiayia a nudge.

They stepped inside, and Pru stood at the door. Mrs. Macdonald followed so she could watch, and then Pru felt a familiar arm around her waist.

"Prudie," Teagan whispered, using her favorite BFF nickname. "I sucked today."

Pru threw her a smile. "We all suck sometimes, Teag. It's fine."

"It's actually not fine, but I love you for saying that." She added a squeeze. "I hate that we're leaving. I'm going to miss you more than anything. I kinda can't bear it. I think it's why I was so cold. I'm really sorry. Really."

"All is forgotten and forgiven, Teag." Pru slipped her arm around Teagan's waist so they were completely connected.

"Are you sure?"

"Positive."

Teag sighed. "And what about UNC in three years? Can we still do that?"

"Of course." Pru gave her a squeeze, all the bad feelings of the day disappearing like yesterday's snow. "Dorm roommates, just like we planned."

"Ho ho ho!" Yiayia's noisy exclamation was accompanied by a loud bark from Charis and a noisy jingle of sleigh bells. Stepping inside, Pru and Teagan huddled close to Mrs. Macdonald so they could all watch from the living room doorway.

Gramma stepped back and let Yiayia kneel in front of the sofa where little Avery was sound asleep.

"Ho ho ho, what do we have here?" she asked in a fake low voice, keeping it soft so she wouldn't scare the girl. But Charis jumped right up on the sofa and started licking her face, making Avery jerk in surprise.

"Merry Christmas, Avery," Yiayia said in her Santa voice.

"*What?*" She sat straight up and threw her arms around the dog. "Puppy! It's a puppy!"

"You like him?" Yiayia asked.

"Santa?" She blinked sleep away, but held the dog tight, giggling as he lapped her cheeks.

"And my wife, Mrs. Finnie Claus." Yiayia gestured to Gramma. "We want you to have this special gift."

"Oh, thank you!" She threw her head back and let him lap at her. "Mommy! Mommy! I got my dog!"

"I see that," Mrs. Macdonald said from the doorway, tears rolling down her cheeks.

"What's his name?" Avery asked, petting his head furiously.

"His name is..." Yiayia got a little closer, putting her hand on the dog's head, too. "His name is Rover. Isn't that a wonderful name for a dog?"

"It's perfect!"

"Rover?" Teagan whispered on a giggle. "Seriously?"

"That's his name," Pru said, fighting a lump in her throat. Maybe this wasn't Charis. Maybe Yiayia still had to find her escort to heaven.

"I love Rover!" Avery scrambled up, still holding the dog like he might be taken away, rushing to her mom. "Look, Mommy. I got a doggy! It's the best Christmas ever!"

Mrs. Macdonald hugged them both, and Teagan threw both arms around Pru. "It is the best Christmas, Prudie. I love you."

"I love—oh, wait!" Pru jumped back. "Your present's in the car. Hang on!" She tore outside and down the walk, giving a little laugh when she saw her dad's refurbished minivan—the one she was conceived in—eww—parked a few feet from Mom's car.

"Everything okay?" he called from the driver's seat.

"Perfect," she called back. "Mission just about accomplished. Who all's in there?"

"Half the Kilcannons," she heard her mom call from inside, making her laugh. "We're going straight to Midnight Mass after this. We all got a second wind, babies included."

Pru gave a thumbs-up and lifted the back hatch, grabbing the present Pru had noticed her mother had brought from the office. As she walked in front of the van's lights, she held it up and mouthed, "Thank you," then jogged back to the house. Gramma, Yiayia, and Mrs. M were hugging goodbye while Avery was running in the snow with Char...Rover.

"Merry Christmas, Teag," she said, handing the wrapped box to Teagan, who waited on the walk. "I remembered how much you loved this when we were at the mall in Chestnut Creek."

"The blue sweater?" Teagan angled her head. "Pru. Thank you. And here, this is for you." She handed Pru a tissue-wrapped little package.

"I thought you didn't have a gift."

"They're the dog-covered leggings. My mom got them for me, but I know how much you wanted them."

"Teagan!" Overwhelmed, Pru threw her arms around her best friend. "I will think of you every time I wear them. Thank you."

They hugged some more, until Gramma and Yiayia came to the door to leave.

"Let's let these fine people rest," Gramma whispered.

"We're headed back to the North Pole!" Yiayia called to Avery, cracking them all up.

"I gotta go, Teag. I'll see you this week?"

"Of course."

"And UNC...class of...'27? Promise?"

Teagan gave her one last hug. "Are you kidding? That's just the beginning." She pointed to the grannies, their arms linked as they headed to the car. "Someday, we're going to be exactly like those two. Besties to the very end."

Pru gave her one more heartfelt hug. "I love that idea! Merry Christmas!" She took off and caught up with her grandmothers, waving at Dad and the crew in the van.

Climbing into the back of the car behind Yiayia, she patted the red velvet arm. "Well done, Santa. Now just follow my dad's van. We're all seventy thousand Kilcannons, Mahoneys, and Santorinis going to Midnight Mass."

"I can't wait," she said, just dryly enough for Pru to wonder if it was genuine sentiment or Yiayia sarcasm. For some reason, she kind of thought it was genuine this time.

With one more wave to Teagan, Pru let her head hit the back of the seat with a sigh of complete contentment. "This really is the best Christmas ever." Then she leaned forward and put her hand on Gramma's little shoulder. "Of course, with you, who knows what'll happen next year?"

"Not knowin' is half the fun, lass."

"I think I'll be Santa again," Yiayia said, waving the van in front of her before pulling out.

"Really?" Gramma asked. "You will?"

"Only if I can sing...dachshund through the snow!"

Gramma rang the bells. "With my bells of sleigh."

Pru finished it off, leaning her face right between theirs. "Off to church we go…laughing all the way!"

And Connor Mahoney is next!
Can the Dogmothers find a woman who will finally
settle him down? Of course they will!
It won't be easy but it sure will be fun!

Want to know the release date, see the cover,
and find out the title? Sign up for the newsletter:

www.roxannestclaire.com

Or get daily updates, sneak peeks, and insider
information at the Dogfather Reader Facebook
Group!

www.facebook.com/groups/roxannestclairereaders/

The Dogmothers is a spinoff series of
The Dogfather

Available Now

SIT...STAY...BEG (Book 1)

NEW LEASH ON LIFE (Book 2)

LEADER OF THE PACK (Book 3)

SANTA PAWS IS COMING TO TOWN (Book 4)
(A Holiday Novella)

BAD TO THE BONE (Book 5)

RUFF AROUND THE EDGES (Book 6)

DOUBLE DOG DARE (Book 7)

BARK! THE HERALD ANGELS SING (Book 8)
(A Holiday Novella)

OLD DOG NEW TRICKS (Book 9)

The Dogmothers Series

Available Now

HOT UNDER THE COLLAR (Book 1)

THREE DOG NIGHT (Book 2)

DACHSHUND THROUGH THE SNOW (Book 3)
(A Holiday Novella)

and many more to come!

For a complete list, buy links, and reading order of all my books, visit www.roxannestclaire.com. Be sure to sign up for my newsletter to find out when the next book is released! And join the private Dogfather Facebook group for inside info on all the books and characters, sneak peeks, and a place to share the love of tails and tales!

www.facebook.com/groups/roxannestclairereaders/

A Dogfather/Dogmothers Family Reference Guide

THE KILCANNON FAMILY

Daniel Kilcannon aka *The Dogfather*
Son of Finola (Gramma Finnie) and Seamus
Kilcannon. Married to Annie Harper for 36 years until
her death. Veterinarian, father, and grandfather.
Widowed at opening of series. Married to Katie
Santorini (*Old Dog New Tricks*) with dogs Rusty and
Goldie.

The Kilcannons (from oldest to youngest):

• **Liam** Kilcannon and Andi Rivers (*Leader of the
Pack*) with Christian and Fiona and dog, Jag

• **Shane** Kilcannon and Chloe Somerset (*New Leash
on* Life) with daughter Annabelle and dogs, Daisy and
Ruby

• **Garrett** Kilcannon and Jessie Curtis
(*Sit…Stay…Beg*) with son Patrick and dog, Lola

• **Molly** Kilcannon and Trace Bancroft (*Bad to the
Bone*) with daughter Pru and son Danny and dog,
Meatball

• **Aidan** Kilcannon and Beck Spencer (*Ruff Around
the Edges*) with dog, Ruff

• **Darcy** Kilcannon and Josh Ranier (*Double Dog
Dare*) with dogs, Kookie and Stella

THE MAHONEY FAMILY

Colleen Mahoney

Daughter of Finola (Gramma Finnie) and Seamus Kilcannon and younger sister of Daniel. Married to Joe Mahoney for a little over 10 years until his death. Owner of Bone Appetit (canine treat bakery) and mother.

The Mahoneys (from oldest to youngest):

• **Declan** Mahoney and…

• **Connor** Mahoney and…

• **Braden** Mahoney and **Cassie** Santorini (*Hot Under the Collar*) with dogs, Jelly Bean and Jasmine

• **Ella** Mahoney and…

THE SANTORINI FAMILY

Katie Rogers Santorini

Dated **Daniel** Kilcannon in college and introduced him to Annie. Married to Nico Santorini for forty years until his death two years after Annie's. Interior Designer and mother. Recently married to **Daniel** Kilcannon (*Old Dogs New Tricks*).

The Santorinis

• **Nick** Santorini and…

• **John** Santorini (identical twin to Alex) and…

• **Alex** Santorini (identical twin to John) and Grace Donovan (*Three Dog Night*) with dogs, Bitsy, Gertie and Jack

• **Theo** Santorini and…

• **Cassie** Santorini and **Braden** Mahoney (*Hot Under the Collar*) with dogs, Jelly Bean and Jasmine

Katie's mother-in-law from her first marriage, **Agnes "Yiayia" Santorini,** now lives in Bitter Bark with **Gramma Finnie** and their dachshunds, Pygmalion (Pyggie) and Galatea (Gala). These two women are known as "The Dogmothers."

About The Author

Published since 2003, Roxanne St. Claire is a *New York Times* and *USA Today* bestselling author of more than fifty romance and suspense novels. She has written several popular series, including The Dogfather, Barefoot Bay, the Guardian Angelinos, and the Bullet Catchers.

In addition to being a ten-time nominee and one-time winner of the prestigious RITA™ Award for the best in romance writing, Roxanne has won the National Readers' Choice Award for best romantic suspense four times. Her books have been published in dozens of languages and optioned for film.

A mother of two but recent empty-nester, Roxanne lives in Florida with her husband and her two dogs, Ginger and Rosie.

www.roxannestclaire.com
www.twitter.com/roxannestclaire
www.facebook.com/roxannestclaire

Made in the USA
Middletown, DE
01 November 2020